FROM HELL TO HEAVEN

Kistna straightened herself and turned to look at the water beneath her. With a shock of sheer horror the Marquis realized what she intended to do.

He reached her in a few strides and when he was beside her and his hands went out to take hold of her, she gave a little cry.

"No ... no! Go ... away! Leave me alone ... you are not to ... stop me!"

The Marquis's arms tightened about her. "Why should you want to do anything so crazy and so utterly and completely mad?"

As if she knew any further struggle would be futile, she suddenly went limp and her head rested against his shoulder.

As he looked down at her, he could see the unhappiness in her eyes and the tear stains on her cheeks. She had changed and become very different from the miserable starving creature who he had thought at first was so ugly.

Now she had a beauty that was different from anything he had seen in any other woman and as he felt her trembling, he knew that never before in his whole life had he felt as he was feeling now.

Her eyes looked into his, and in a broken little voice she whispered: "I ... I ... love you ... I ... cannot ... help it ... I love ... you."

Bantam Books by Barbara Cartland
Ask your bookseller for the titles you have missed

Barbara Cartland's Library of Love Series

Books of Love and Revelation

Other books by Barbara Cartland

From Hell
to
Heaven

Barbara Cartland

BANTAM BOOKS · LONDON
TORONTO · NEW YORK

FROM HELL TO HEAVEN
A Bantam Book / January 1981

ISBN 0–553–14361–1

Published simultaneously in the United States and Canada

Bantam Books are published by Bantam Books, Inc. Its trade-
mark, consisting of the words "Bantam Books" and the por-
trayal of a bantam, is Registered in U.S. Patent and Trademark
Office and in other countries. Marca Registrada. Bantam
Books, Inc., 666 Fifth Avenue, New York, New York 10103.

PRINTED IN THE UNITED STATES OF AMERICA

0 9 8 7 6 5 4 3 2 1

Author's Note

A dead-heat at the Derby Stakes begins this tale of love and hate, misery and happiness. There have actually been two dead-heats at the "Blue Riband of the Turf," the greatest horse-race in the world.

In 1828 the Duke of Rutland's *Cadland* dead-heated with *The Colonel,* owned by the Hon. Edward Petre. Under the then rules of racing, this dead-heat was run off later in the afternoon and *Cadland* won.

One of the most historic Derbies ever run took place in 1884. At the spring meeting at Newmarket, the Prince of Batthyány was in a high state of excitement as *Galliard,* a son of his much-loved *Galopin,* was expected to win the two thousand guineas. However, the strain was too much for the Prince, and he had a fatal heart-attack as he entered the Jockey Club luncheon-rooms.

His death undoubtedly altered the course of Turf History, as the classic nomination of his colt *St. Simon* was thereby rendered void according to the rule that then existed. *St. Simon* proved to be the greatest race-horse ever and certainly the greatest Sire ever known to the English Turf. There is no doubt that he would have won the 1884 Derby.

In his absence, the race resulted in a dead-heat between Sir John Willoughby's *Harvester* and Mr. John Hammond's *St. Gatien.* The Stewards gave the owners the option of having a run-off or dividing the race, and they unanimously decided to divide.

Chapter One

1831

There had been a long wait, as was usual with a big field, then a number of false starts.

The Marquis of Alchester, with his glasses trained on the horses in the far distance, gave an impatient sigh.

"Feeling anxious, Linden?" Peregrine Wallingham asked.

"No, merely confident," the Marquis replied, and his friend laughed.

"That is exactly what Branscombe says."

The Marquis's expression darkened.

He was well aware that the Earl of Branscombe's *Gunpowder* was a definite danger to his own *Highflyer*, but, as he had just said, he was confident that his horse would be the winner.

The huge crowd sprawling over the hill was, as usual on Derby Day, different from the crowd at any other race-meeting.

The Derby Stakes, which was the Blue Riband of the Turf, was a day to which all sportsmen looked forward, and although it was not an official holiday there was hardly an employer in the country who did not expect his employees to absent themselves if they were anywhere within reach of Epsom.

"They're off!"

The cry went up with a big shout as the flag was down and the horses began the long run which led them round Tattenham Corner and up the straight in front of the stands.

This was a golden opportunity for pick-pockets, for necks were craned and the attention of everybody was on the horses.

In less than three minutes it would all be over, and confirmation of the race result would be signalled by a flight of pigeons circling up over the stands and carrying the name of the winner to the newspapers and bookies in different parts of the country.

There were roars from the crowd all along the course.

In the stand of the Jockey Club, where the more important owners watched their own horses and those they had backed with a concentration that had no need for audible expression, there was silence.

Peregrine Wallingham was aware that on this occasion there was an extra tension owing to the rivalry between the Earl of Branscombe and the Marquis of Alchester.

They were old enemies, and because he was the Marquis's oldest and closest friend he disliked the Earl almost as much as the Marquis did.

One reason was that the Earl of Branscombe considered himself not only the finest sportsman in the country but of such importance that he conceded that only the King took precedence over him.

Dukes, Marquises, and other Earls he dismissed with a wave of his hand, and asserted with some truth that his blood and his ancient title made him superior to them and that it was only due to some quirk of fate that he was not in fact a candidate for the Throne itself!

What was so infuriating, especially for the Marquis, was the fact that there was justification for the Earl's assertions and he was indeed outstanding and exceptionally fortunate in the Sporting World.

Certainly his horses had in the last two years won many of the classic races, but then so had those belonging to the Marquis.

Both gentlemen were exceptional shots and outstanding amateur pugilists, and both could speak in the House of Lords so eloquently that their fellow Peers flocked into the Chamber to hear them, especially when they were opposing each other.

But while the Marquis was popular with his contemporaries, the Earl was not. Although both habitually gave themselves airs, the Earl was, everybody decided behind his back, almost intolerable.

Now the horses had rounded Tattenham Corner and were coming at a good pace up the last stretch of the course.

When there was a large field it was difficult to see exactly which was ahead until they drew nearer.

Then as the crowd began to chant the names it was easy to hear the cry of *"Gunpowder! Gunpowder!"* being drowned by the roaring of *"Highflyer! Highflyer!"*

They drew nearer, and Peregrine Wallingham murmured beneath his breath:

"My God, it is going to be a close finish!"

He knew that the Marquis at his side was aware of it too, not from anything he said, but because of a sudden rigidity about his long, athletic body.

Then on the other side of him Peregrine Wallingham heard the Earl mutter impatiently:

"Come on, blast you!"

Now the cries of the crowd grew louder, and as the horses drew nearer, Peregrine Wallingham realized that the two in the lead were riding literally neck and neck.

It was impossible to guess which one would pass the Winning-Post first.

The jockeys had their whips raised, but there was really no need to use them. Both horses were aware that they had to best the other and were striving with every muscle in their bodies to get ahead.

Then as they flashed past the Post there was a sudden sound which those familiar with racing knew was one of astonishment.

For the second time in fifty years, the Derby Stakes seemed to have finished in a dead-heat.

"Mine by a nose, I think!" the Earl said aggressively, taking his glasses from his eyes.

The Marquis did not deign to answer. He merely turned and walked from the Box, followed by his friend Peregrine Wallingham, and they hurried through the crowds to the gate through which the horses, when they had been pulled in, would leave the course.

"I have never seen anything so extraordinary!" Peregrine exclaimed as he walked beside the Marquis.

"I do not believe there was an inch between them," the Marquis replied, "whatever Branscombe may pretend!"

"You are right," Peregrine agreed. "At the same time, it is a pity you could not have won. Branscombe has been boasting for the last month that his horse was a sure winner, and I am certain in consequence he has shortened the odds."

The Marquis gave his friend a sharp glance.

"You surely did not back *Gunpowder?*"

"Of course not," Peregrine replied. "I put my shirt on *Highflyer,* but unfortunately I had not much of it left."

The Marquis laughed.

"You should stick to horses," he said. "In the long run they are cheaper than Cyprians."

"I found that out a long time ago," Peregrine agreed. "But that little dancer from the Covent Garden has a magnet which makes the guineas fly out of my pocket quicker than I can put them in!"

He spoke ruefully, but the Marquis was not listening.

He was watching his horse trotting back down the course and was aware that his jockey was having a violent altercation with the rider of the Earl's *Gunpowder.*

Only when the noise of the crowd cheering them from behind the rails made it impossible for them to hear each other could they concentrate on riding triumphantly through the lane cleared for them towards the Weighing-In Room.

As the horses entered the enclosure the Marquis

was waiting and when his jockey dismounted he said to him:

"What happened, Bennett?"

"Bumped an' obstructed me 'e did, when we was coming into the straight after rounding Tattenham Corner, M'Lord. I'd have beat him easy, but for that!"

The Marquis was scowling.

"Is this true?" he asked. "You are sure of what you are saying?"

"'E were behavin' as bad as be possible for a rider t' act, M'Lord, an' that's th' truth."

"I believe you," the Marquis said, "but I doubt if there is anything we can do about it. Get weighed in."

Carrying his saddle, the jockey went towards the Weighing-In machine, which the Stewards were supervising, and as he reached it the Earl's jockey passed him with a grin on his face.

As he did so he said in a voice only he could hear:

"Squeaking, are ye? Won't do ye no good!"

Bennett had been warned by the Marquis in the past not to brawl or to enter into arguments in front of the Stewards.

Right or wrong, it always reflected on both of those concerned, and although Bennett pressed his lips together in what was almost a grimace, he said nothing.

Only when he rejoined the Marquis did he say:

"I'll get that Jake Smith if it's th' last thing I does! 'E rides dirty an' that's why no-one w'd employ 'im till His Lordship took 'im on."

The Marquis's eyes narrowed.

"Is that a fact?" he enquired.

"'Tis well known, M'Lord. Jake Smith were beggin' for a ride till three months ago."

The Marquis did not speak for a moment. Then he congratulated his jockey, promised the usual reward which was a very generous one for riding the winner, and rejoined Peregrine Wallingham.

He told him what he had heard, and Peregrine said:

"I heard that Smith was a questionable jockey before he was taken on by Branscombe, but he has never ridden a horse that I would wish to back. I will find out what I can about him, Linden."

"Do that," the Marquis agreed, "but now, I think, unless you particularly want to stay for the next race, we should be getting back to London. The crowds are going to make it an exhausting journey and the quicker we get away from the course the better."

"I am ready to go," Peregrine Wallingham replied.

"What is more," the Marquis went on, "I have no wish to return to the Box and hear Branscombe averring, which he is sure to do, that he is in reality the winner."

"It has been officially declared a dead-heat," Peregrine said, "so you share the prize money—twenty-eight hundred pounds."

"That will not prevent him from saying I am not entitled to it," the Marquis said grimly. "God, how I dislike that man!"

Peregrine laughed.

"That is obvious, and I admit his conceit and bumptiousness gets under everybody's skin, except of course the Monarch's."

The Marquis said nothing.

He was only too well aware that the new King, William IV, had been beguiled by the Earl's inflated estimation of his own abilities into thinking him an exceptionally good advisor.

The Earl had jumped at the chance, and as a Courtier had said somewhat bitterly:

"I have always found one Monarch enough, but when one has two of them, I find my position almost insupportable!"

Trusting, good-natured, and rather stupid, the King was anxious to make a good impression on his subjects, and with the help of his dowdy and dull little German wife to have a very different Court from that of his brother, George IV.

He had swept away the immorality and raffishness of the Court which had scandalised the country, but unfortunately the laughter had gone too, as those who attended the King at Windsor, Buckingham Palace, and Windsor Castle were sometimes dismayed to find.

The Princess de Lieven, wife of the Russian Ambassador, had complained to the Marquis that the Court was now intolerably dreary and dull.

"There is no possibility of even having a reasonable conversation," she had said bitterly. "In the evening we all sit at a round table. The King snoozes, and the Queen does needlework, and talks with great animation but with never a word of politics."

The Marquis had laughed.

He knew that the Princess, who was vivacious, witty, and usually very indiscreet, was undoubtedly suffering, and he only hoped that the Earl of Branscombe was finding his self-appointed position a bore.

Actually, when the Marquis was alone with the King he found him, although inclined to be repetitive, quite interesting on subjects on which he was an authority.

But he had in many ways to agree with the Duke of Wellington, who had said in his blunt manner:

"Really, my master is too stupid! When at table he wishes to make a speech, I always turn to him my deaf ear so as not to be tempted to contradict him."

The Marquis began to move swiftly through the crowd of touts, gypsies, confidence men, and beggars.

There were dwarfs, clowns, acrobats, minstrels, and tipsters, all of whom added to the hubbub of the occasion.

As quickly as was possible the Marquis found his Phaeton, and as soon as he was driving his horses in the direction of London, Peregrine said:

"I presume the King, who knows little about racing, will be pleased that Branscombe's horse came in first, even if he is forced to share the honour and glory with you."

"Doubtless the King will believe that Branscombe would have won if *Highflyer* had not passed the Winning-Post at the same moment by a sheer fluke!"

The Marquis spoke bitterly and Peregrine was aware that the result rankled.

Actually, he thought it had been very exciting and certainly a surprise which few race-goers would have expected.

Because he was genuinely fond of the Marquis, he said consolingly:

"Well, you and I, Linden, know that he only won by a foul, but it will not do any good to say so."

"No, of course not," the Marquis agreed, "but I will do my best to see that damned jockey gets his deserts. I bet you any money you like that Branscombe knew what he was doing when he engaged the man."

"Of course he did!" Peregrine agreed. "He was determined to beat you by fair means or foul."

"That does not surprise me," the Marquis said. "Branscombe has always been the same ever since he was at Eton. He has to be top, and, if you remember, even there we were always running neck and neck for some position or other."

Peregrine laughed.

The rivalry between the two boys had been the talk of the School and the other scholars had divided themselves equally behind one or the other. It had been very much the same when they had both gone to Oxford.

He himself had always disliked the Earl because he knew that despite his success in the field of sport, he was fundamentally unsporting.

He was not averse to taking an underhanded advantage in any contest, and he intended always to be the winner.

Some boys and young men sense with an almost clairvoyant perception the flaws in each other, and Peregrine had always been quite sure that somewhere in the Earl there was a canker of which few people were aware.

The Marquis was different.

Although he had his faults, he was in his friend's mind a gentleman who would never do anything that was not completely straight and honourable.

"What are you thinking about?" the Marquis enquired as they cleared the worst of the crowds and the horses were able to move more quickly.

"You, as it happens."

"I am flattered!" the Marquis said sarcastically. "But why?"

"I was comparing you to Branscombe, to his disadvantage."

"So I should think, and I am not looking forward to the dinner this evening."

The Derby Dinner given by the Stewards of the Jockey Club was always an important occasion, and every winner of the Derby enjoyed the congratulations and the honour that was accorded to him on that particular evening.

It would be particularly irksome, as Peregrine knew, for the Marquis to have to pretend that he enjoyed the Earl's company and to repress the knowledge that their horses had been equal owing only to foul riding by his jockey.

"Let us hope we need not stay long," Peregrine said in an effort to cheer up his friend. "There are some very attractive little 'bits of muslin' arrived from France at the Palace of Pleasure, whom you may find interesting, as soon as we can get away."

The Marquis did not reply. Peregrine remembered that his friend usually found such Houses a waste of time, and he said quickly:

"But I expect you have arranged to meet Lady Isobel."

There was just a note of doubt in the question, as if he realised that recently the Marquis had not been seen with Lady Isobel Sidley as often as might have been expected.

This was surprising, for she was not only an acknowledged beauty in London Society but was also quite obviously wildly, passionately in love with the Marquis to the point where the whole Social World was aware of it.

Lady Isobel had, Peregrine often thought, been born too late. Her impetuous indiscretions were such as had been admired fifteen years ago by the Regent.

He had loved pretty women and he had certainly not wished them to be moral or prudent.

Unfortunately, Lady Isobel had never learnt to control her feelings, and her infatuation for the Marquis, which she had made no attempt to disguise, had already shocked the Queen.

There was a distinct pause. Then with his eyes on his horses the Marquis said:

"No. I shall not be seeing Isobel. To tell you the truth, Peregrine, I am no longer interested."

His friend turned to stare at him incredulously.

He had thought that perhaps the Marquis might remonstrate with Isobel or curtail some of the time they were seen together in public, but that he should have finished with her completely was incredible.

"Do you really mean that?" he enquired.

The Marquis nodded.

"I am bored."

There was no obvious reply to that, and again there was silence as they drove on.

Peregrine was thinking that it was typical of the Marquis to be so ruthless in making a decision which most men in his position would find hard to implement.

But the Marquis was very blunt, and, if he was bored, whoever was boring him would be shown the door immediately, and there would be no appeal against his decision to finish either a love-affair or a friendship.

"Does Isobel know this?" Peregrine asked at length.

"I have not yet told her in so many words," the Marquis replied, "though I intend to do so when the opportunity arises. But I think she must have some inkling, as we have not seen each other for over a week."

Peregrine remembered seeing a groom in Sidley

livery delivering a letter at the Marquis's house when he had been with him that morning.

He was certain that Lady Isobel would be very voluble on paper if she could not get the chance of saying what she thought in person.

Suddenly he saw storm-clouds ahead, and he only hoped that he would not be involved in them.

Then as if he knew that this was the moment when he must tell the Marquis what was on his mind and what had been worrying him considerably all day, he said:

"Are you ready to hear something which will annoy you?"

The way he spoke, rather than what he said, made the Marquis look at him sharply.

"Does it concern Isobel?"

"No, it has nothing to do with her," Peregrine said quickly. "It is something I feel I have to tell you, and I have been waiting for a propitious moment."

"Which you think is now?"

"I suppose it is as good a time as any," Peregrine said a little ruefully. "As a matter of fact, I was remembering that in the old days Kings cut off the heads of messengers who brought them bad news."

The Marquis laughed.

"Is that what you are afraid will happen to you?"

"At least for the moment your hands are engaged with the reins!" Peregrine replied.

The Marquis laughed again.

"I will not hit you, you fool, whatever you tell me, and now that you have aroused my curiosity I am naturally speculating as to what it can be."

"It concerns Branscombe."

The Marquis groaned.

"I am trying to forget him before I have to see his smug face at the dinner tonight."

"According to him, Her Majesty admires him enormously and thinks he looks just as a gentleman should."

"God help us!" the Marquis ejaculated. "And incidentally, Branscombe does not consider himself a gentleman but a nobleman, which entitles him to be more self-satisfied, more blown up with his own importance, and more bumptious than he is already!"

"It is a pity we cannot tell him so," Peregrine said, laughing.

"What are you going to tell me about him that I do not know already?"

"I will be surprised if you do!" Peregrine remarked. "You are aware that the Queen is anxious that those who are in attendance at Court should be 'properly and respectably' married?"

"The Princess de Lieven told me," the Earl replied, "that the Queen said: 'We want all those dear people who are closest to the King to be as happy and compatible as we are.'"

The way the Marquis mimicked the Queen's voice made it sound sickly sentimental, and Peregrine said quickly:

"Be careful, Linden, or Her Majesty will have you up the aisle before you are aware of it!"

"I assure you she will do nothing of the sort!" the Marquis retorted. "I have no hesitation in declaring that I have no intention of marrying any woman before I wish to do so, even if for disobeying the Royal Command I am sent to the Tower!"

"That I can well believe," Peregrine smiled, "but Branscombe has agreed with the Queen that it is an excellent idea and has already mentioned privately to one or two people the name of the woman he intends to marry."

The way Peregrine spoke told the Marquis that what he was saying was significant, and because he knew it was expected of him, he asked:

"I presume you intend to tell me who the unfortunate female is?"

"The Princess de Lieven told me in confidence, because she said she was too frightened to tell you herself," Peregrine replied, "that Branscombe intends to marry your Ward as soon as she arrives in England."

The expression on the Marquis's face was one of sheer astonishment.

"My Ward!" he exclaimed. "Who the devil . . . ?"

He stopped.

"You cannot mean Mirabelle?"

"Exactly! Mirabelle Chester!"

"But the girl is still at School. She has seen nothing of the world, and anyway she is not arriving in England for another month."

"That is true," Peregrine agreed, "but naturally people have been talking about her."

"By which you mean," the Marquis said sharply, "that they have been talking about her fortune!"

"As usual, you have hit the nail on the head!"

The Marquis gave an exclamation that was almost an oath.

"You are not telling me that Branscombe needs money?"

"The Princess told me, again in confidence," Peregrine replied, "that he has secretly been looking for an heiress for some time. Apparently he said to someone who reported it to the Princess that, much as he disliked you, he could not deny that the Chester blood was nearly compatible with his own!"

The Marquis exploded.

"Nearly, indeed!"

"When he heard of the extent of your Ward's fortune," Peregrine went on, "he decided that she is exactly what he needs."

The Marquis's lips tightened before he asked:

"But for Heaven's sake, why?"

"I gathered, from the Princess's rather garbled explanation, that he found on his father's death that the old Earl had not left him all he expected."

"He will marry her over my dead body!" the Marquis exclaimed. "As Mirabelle's Guardian, I would never give my permission for her to marry Branscombe."

There was silence. Then Peregrine said:

"You will have to give substantial grounds for your refusal."

The Marquis did not answer for a moment, but his friend knew by the expression on his face that he was realising it would be very difficult for any Guardian to refuse the Earl of Branscombe as a suitor.

Whatever might be felt about him privately, publicly he was the holder of a great and honoured title, the possessor of an Estate that, like his ancestors, was part of the history of England, and he certainly enjoyed the favour of both the King and the Queen.

The Marquis had already considered his responsibilities towards the daughter of his first cousin.

Edward Chester, who had died two years ago, had been one of those brilliant but restless people who was happy only when he was exploring strange parts of the world or risking his life quite unnecessarily in adventures that would have appalled more-cautious men.

Although his travels had often been extremely uncomfortable and dangerous, in the course of them he had become enormously wealthy.

Someone who had befriended him had left him shares in a gold-mine which had suddenly borne fruit, and in another part of the world, land he had written off as a dead loss had become valuable overnight when oil was found in it.

Perhaps because he was not particularly interested in stocks and shares, those he had bought in a haphazard fashion always seemed to bloom the minute he acquired them.

When he was killed, as everybody expected he would be, attempting to cross a range of mountains which were considered impassable, his daughter Mirabelle found herself to be the possessor of a huge fortune and a Guardian to administer it for her whom she had never even seen.

Mirabelle's mother had been half-Italian, and when Edward Chester had left on his last expedition, from which he had never returned, he had deposited his wife and daughter in Italy.

It was unlikely that the letter which had been despatched to him telling him of his wife's death had ever reached him, and the Marquis had learnt first of Mrs. Chester's death, then of his cousin Edward's, within a month of each other.

All this had happened last summer, and while he

was wondering what he should do he had received a letter from Mirabelle's aunt with whom she was staying in Italy.

The Contessa told him that as her niece was attending an excellent School in Rome, she thought it would be a mistake for her to come to England until she was out of mourning.

The Marquis had agreed.

"Next year, when she is eighteen," he had told Peregrine, "she can be presented to the Queen, and I have plenty of relatives who will be only too pleased to chaperone her."

"Are you also going to sit on the dais with all the Dowagers?" Peregrine had teased.

"I am not going to do anything except fight off the fortune-hunters," the Marquis had replied. "By God, Peregrine, do you know how much this girl owns?"

When he heard the answer to this question, Peregrine had agreed with the Marquis that it was far too much for one young woman and would undoubtedly result in all the wasters swarming round her like hornets.

"I am going to marry her off to the first decent man who comes along, then I shall be free of responsibility," the Marquis had said. "Because I was fond of Edward, eccentric though he was, I will not let his daughter be imposed on by one of those titled ne'er-do-wells who think all a rich woman wants from them is a coronet."

Those sentiments were extremely laudable, Peregrine was thinking now. At the same time, nobody could say that the Earl of Branscombe was a ne'er-do-well and had nothing to offer except a title.

Peregrine was aware that the Marquis was determined not to inflict a man he loathed and despised on the daughter of his cousin for whom he had had an affection.

But it was going to be extremely difficult to think of a plausible refusal which would not result in the Earl causing a scandal by immediately calling him out.

William IV had expressly forbidden duelling, but where there was a will there was a way, and in certain circumstances gentlemen could, if they wished, settle their differences by the time-honoured method of firing at each other, without there being any scandal.

It was difficult to know who, if such a duel did take place, would be the winner, but it was something Peregrine knew must be prevented at all costs.

Aloud he said:

"I know exactly what you are feeling, Linden, but if Branscombe has set his heart on marrying your Ward, it is going to be damned difficult to prevent him from doing so."

The Marquis's lips tightened before he said:

"It is just like him to say he is going to marry a woman without having the courtesy to ask her first!"

"He knows only too well that no girl would refuse him," Peregrine replied. "The Earl of Branscombe, the highest in the land, the King's favourite! It would be a fairy-tale come true!"

"Except that you and I know under all that tinsel he is not Prince Charming or ever likely to be."

Peregrine nodded.

"Do you remember Rosie?"

The Marquis did not reply, but they were both thinking of the little dancer whom the Earl had deliberately seduced away from the Marquis when he was out of London attending a race-meeting in the North.

On his return he found that the Earl had installed her in a far larger house than the one he had provided for her, with now four horses instead of two for her carriage, and her jewellery was dazzling.

Knowing that it was a deliberate way of scoring off him, the Marquis had been annoyed, but because he had been too clever to show his annoyance the Earl did not have the satisfaction out of the episode that he had expected.

In fact, the Marquis had said openly in the Club, knowing it would be repeated, that he was extremely grateful to the Earl for relieving him of a young

woman who he had already found had a very small
repertoire and none of it worth repeating.

What he had not expected was that his and the
Earl's animosity towards each other had ended the
girl's career.

Because he was annoyed by the Marquis's reaction, the Earl had deliberately taken his revenge on
her.

He had not only deprived her of everything he
had given her, which was against all the rules of such
liaisons, but he had gone out of his way to see that she
was dismissed from the Theatre and was unable to
find any engagements elsewhere.

She had come to see the Marquis in desperation
because she was actually almost starving.

She had been afraid that he would punish her for
the way she had treated him, and she had appealed to
him only as a last resort.

The Marquis had not only been extremely generous but had got her an engagement in a touring-
company playing the larger towns in the Provinces in
a show which had eventually come to London.

He was no longer interested in her as a woman,
and he would not have stooped to pick up the Earl's
leavings, but she had thanked him for his kindness
with tears in her eyes.

The Marquis had merely added another notch on
the tally he was marking up against his enemy.

Now he said with an urgent note in his voice:

"What am I to do, Peregrine? You have to help
me with this."

"I want to," Peregrine replied, "but how can we
set about it?"

"We could, of course, write to the Contessa and
ask her to keep Mirabelle in Italy and not let her come
to London this Season."

"Surely that will only be postponing the evil
hour? And if Branscombe has made up his mind to
marry her, he might even go out to Rome."

The Marquis drove on and they must have travelled for nearly half-an-hour before he said:

"There must be something we can do!"

"Only find him another heiress!" Peregrine replied. "And there are not many girls about as rich as Mirabelle Chester."

"I know," the Marquis agreed, "and although I have not seen her since she was a baby, I am told she is pretty and has a sweet nature."

"I do not suppose Branscombe is particularly interested in her nature," Peregrine said cynically.

"I have to stop this marriage," the Marquis snapped. "If Edward were alive he would whisk her off to the top of the Himalayas or across the Gobi Desert. But personally I should be unable to look after myself in such outlandish places, let alone a young girl!"

"There must be something we can do," Peregrine repeated. "There must be other heiresses in London waiting to make their curtseys to the Queen."

"If there was anybody outstanding we would have heard about her," the Marquis said, "and certainly the Princess de Lieven would know. There is not a piece of gossip in circulation small enough to escape her sharp ears!"

"Shall we ask her?" Peregrine suggested.

"For God's sake, no!" the Marquis ejaculated. "I swear Branscombe shall not marry my Ward, but you know as well as I do that the Princess would not be able to resist telling him I had said so, which would make him more determined than ever."

"I do not suppose anything will stop him," Peregrine said, "not if he really wants money. And if it comes to that, who does not really want money except you?"

"We are talking about Mirabelle," the Marquis said, as if he felt he must keep to the point. "I suppose I could persuade her to say she would not accept him."

"That is all very well," Peregrine said, "but you know perfectly well that all your relatives would think it a splendid match. Among the available eligible bachelors, compared to Branscombe there is no-one as suitable except yourself, and you can hardly marry your own Ward."

"You are right about that," the Marquis said. "Besides, I have no intention of marrying anyone, especially not an unfledged School-girl."

"Then we are back to where we started," Peregrine said, "with Branscombe the villain or the hero of the piece, whichever way you like to look at him, and the heroine, young, unsophisticated, sweet, and innocent, with no idea what she is in for as she walks into the arena!"

He spoke dramatically, expecting the Marquis to laugh.

Instead he said sharply:

"Say that again!"

"Say what?"

"What you said just now. It gave me an idea!"

"I said: 'with Brans—'"

"No, not him. What you said about the girl."

"I said: 'and the heroine, young, unsophisticated, sweet, and innocent,'" Peregrine repeated slowly.

"That is it!" the Marquis exclaimed. "That is it! And Branscombe has never seen her!"

"What are you talking about?"

"It is obvious. All we have to do is find a young, unsophisticated, sweet, and innocent girl to take the place of my Ward. Branscombe will propose to her because she is rich. But it does not have to be Mirabelle! He will only think it is she."

"Are you suggesting that you produce a fake Mirabelle," Peregrine asked, "and palm her off on Branscombe as your Ward?"

"Exactly!" the Marquis said. "That is what I intend to do! If he can cheat me and my horses out of winning the Derby Stakes, I can cheat him when it comes to his winning his future wife!"

"You may have an idea there," Peregrine conceded, "but whom do you have in mind?"

"I have no-one at the moment," the Marquis replied, "but we are going to find this 'young, unsophisticated, sweet, and innocent girl' and we are going to groom her secretly in our own stables, so to speak, until we think she is ready for the matrimonial stakes which Branscombe thinks is going to be a walkover!"

"But who will she be?" Peregrine asked.

"That is the crux of the joke," the Marquis said. "I will tell you exactly who she will be."

He paused before with a hard, metallic note in his voice he said:

"Branscombe is a snob, so she will come from the gutter; Branscombe wants money, so she will be penniless; Branscombe wants a blue-blooded wife of whom he can be proud, so she will be a nobody! That will teach him a lesson he will never forget—and nor shall I!"

Chapter Two

"I congratulate you!" Peregrine said as they drove away.

The Marquis, intent on tooling his Phaeton, smiled, which told his friend that everything had gone as he had expected.

Last night when they had arrived at the Marquis's country house in Hertfordshire, they had sat up late, arguing as to whether they would be able to find the type of girl they had in mind with whom to deceive the Earl.

Peregrine had been insistent from the beginning that she would have to be an actress, but the Marquis had said firmly:

"If she was acting it would soon become obvious, and that is something we must avoid at all costs. He has to actually marry our fake before we expose her and make him look a fool."

"I can see your point," Peregrine said reluctantly.

"What is more," the Marquis went on, "I have no intention of laying myself open to an accusation of trickery."

"What do you mean?"

"I mean," the Marquis said firmly, "that whatever girl I produce, she will in fact be my Ward."

Peregrine looked at him in astonishment.

"How do you intend to contrive that?"

The Marquis's lips twisted in a wry smile.

"If I were in the East I could doubtless buy

in a slave-market, but as we are in England we have to acquire her by more subtle means."

"You are not suggesting employing one of those old harridans who entice young girls up from the country into bawdy-houses and sell them to the type of man who likes them young and innocent?"

"I would certainly not sink to that sort of trick," the Marquis said sharply. "But there must be girls who would be only too pleased to have a rich Guardian."

"Orphans, for instance," Peregrine agreed.

The Marquis gave an exclamation.

"That is the answer!" he said. "Of course, orphans, and I maintain two Orphanages."

"Then we must certainly visit them," Peregrine said, "and with no relatives to turn up unexpectedly and make a scene or try to blackmail you, everything should be plane-sailing."

"We first have to choose the orphan," the Marquis remarked.

At the same time he was smiling, and Peregrine had to admit that his idea was a clever one.

All the way driving down to Alchester Abbey they talked of nothing else.

The Marquis's ancestral home, built before the Dissolution of the Monasteries, had been a Cistercian Abbey and architecturally was one of the most beautiful buildings in the whole of Great Britain.

It had been converted into an extremely comfortable house. At the same time, the exquisite Cloisters, the great Refectory, and the medieval Chapel were still there.

Peregrine always thought that Alchester Abbey had an atmosphere that was different from that of any other house in which he had stayed.

He felt it was not something he could say to the Marquis, although he often wondered why the holiness of it did not soften his whole attitude towards the world outside.

There was no doubt that now the Marquis was determined, where the Earl was concerned, to live up to his reputation of being ruthless and at times extremely hard.

Yet the Earl deserved everything that was coming to him.

This was confirmed when, before they left London the morning after the Derby Dinner, the Marquis was told that his jockey would like to speak to him.

"Do you want me to leave you?" Peregrine asked, as they walked from the Breakfast-Room into the Library.

The Marquis shook his head.

"No, I want you to hear what Bennett has to say. It will be useful for me to have a witness, if it is what I suspect."

Peregrine held up his hands in horror.

"I refuse, absolutely refuse, to be involved in your row with Branscombe! He is an unpleasant enemy and I am not up to his weight."

"I am not asking you to fight him," the Marquis said, "I will do that. I merely want your moral support, which I have always had in the past."

"Morally, it is all yours!" Peregrine said with a smile. "Physically, I am inclined to run for cover!"

The Marquis laughed.

"I never thought you were a coward!"

"I simply know when discretion is the better part of valour!"

They were both laughing as the Butler announced:

"Bennett, M'Lord!"

The jockey came into the room looking anxious.

Peregrine thought that without the colours and cap which gave jockeys a certain glamour, in their ordinary clothes they always appeared small and insignificant.

"Good-morning, Bennett!" the Marquis said. "I hope, as you are here, that my secretary has given you the reward you were promised."

"Yes, M'Lord, and I'm very grateful, M'Lord, considering I were only entitled to half o' what you've given I."

"I thought you rode an excellent race, Bennett, and did the best you could in the circumstances."

"Which is what I wanted to speak about to Your Lordship."

"I am listening," the Marquis said.

"After th' meeting was over, Smith were a-drinking with 'is pals, and having been watching 'is weight before th' race, 'e has a few over the odds, so to speak."

"So he was drunk," the Marquis said.

"Yes, M'Lord, and 'e were a-talkin' free-like."

"What did he say?"

"That 'e were resentful, M'Lord, as 'e'd been told that as 'e hadn't won as 'e'd been instructed to do, 'e'd receive no extra fee."

The Marquis stiffened.

"Are you seriously telling me, Bennett, that the Earl of Branscombe is not giving Smith anything extra for carrying his horse past the Winning-Post, even though it was a dead-heat?"

"That's what 'e says, M'Lord," Bennett confirmed. "'E were a-grumblin' that 'twere a mean action on th' part o' 'is Lordship, considerin' 'e'd done 'is best to carry out 'is instructions."

"Did he say what they were?"

"'E made that clear enough, M'Lord," Bennett answered. "As 'e were a-leavin' 'e comes across to me an' says:

"''Tis yer fault, Bennett, that I'm skint. Next time I'll take me whip, as 'is Lordship tells I, ter ye and yer damned 'orse.'"

"What was your reply?" the Marquis enquired.

"I didn't get a chance to say anythin', M'Lord. Two of the Branscombe grooms was there with 'im. They realised 'e were sayin' things in 'is cups 'e wouldn't say out loud if 'e were sober, an' they 'ustled 'im away."

The Marquis was silent for a moment, then he said:

"Thank you, Bennett, you have told me exactly what I expected, and I am glad to have it confirmed. I shall offer you the choice of the three horses I am

entering for the races at Ascot. I feel sure that if
things go well, you will make certain of the Gold Cup
for me."

Bennett's grin stretched from ear to ear.

"Thank ye, M'Lord. Thank ye very much! It's a
chance I've always wanted. And I'd rather ride fer
Your Lordship than any other owner; ye've always
been fair and square and no rider can ask more than
that."

The jockey was smiling when he left the Library,
and the Marquis turned to Peregrine.

"You heard what he said. Branscombe deliberately told his jockey to prevent my horse from winning
the race."

"There is nothing you can do about it now,"
Peregrine said. "If Bennett repeated what he just said
in front of the Stewards, his word would not be taken
against that of Branscombe, who would obviously
deny it."

"I am aware of that," the Marquis said. "That is
why I have no compunction about playing a trick on
him which will definitely not be as unsporting as what
he tried to do to me."

"There I agree with you," Peregrine replied, "but
it is not going to be easy."

However, they set out from the Abbey to visit the
Marquis's Orphanages with the hope that there they
would find exactly the right type of young girl who,
with careful grooming, would be able to deceive the
Earl.

On most important Estates the owner in some
century or another had built Orphanages and Alms
Houses.

The Marquis explained that the newest one,
which they were to visit first, had been built by his
grandmother.

"My grandfather was an extremely raffish character with a large number of love-children. I always felt
that my grandmother meant it as some reparation for
his sins."

"If you are expecting to find one of your relations
from the wrong side of the blanket there, I think you

will be unlucky," Peregrine remarked. "They would be too long in the tooth to pass off on Branscombe as suitable young women."

"I know that," the Marquis replied. "I was just explaining to you why this particular Orphanage was built, and it is, I have always understood, a model of its kind."

It was apparent that the Marquis had not spoken idly.

The Orphanage was attractive to look at, and the orphans, about twenty of them, seemed healthy and happy.

The Matron, a motherly woman, was delighted and a little overcome by the Marquis's visit.

She showed them with justifiable pride that everything was clean and tidy, and the orphans themselves showed good manners in their bows and curtseys.

There was, however, one snag which both the Marquis and Peregrine realised immediately.

All the orphans were very young, and when he commented on it, the Matron explained:

"As soon as the orphans reach the age of twelve, M'Lord, they leave; the boys are apprenticed to a trade, the girls are sent into Domestic Service."

"At twelve years of age!" the Marquis exclaimed.

"Yes, M'Lord. I sent my two eldest girls up to the Abbey a month ago, and I understand they are doing well in the scullery."

The Marquis glanced at Peregrine and they both knew their visit had been fruitless.

Having pleased the Matron by his expressions of approval, the Marquis climbed back into his Phaeton, and as the groom released the horses' heads and jumped up behind, they drove off.

"It was a good idea," Peregrine said, "but how were we to know the orphans are disposed of as soon as they are old enough to work?"

"Do you suppose that is true of all Orphanages?" the Marquis asked.

"I expect so," Peregrine answered.

"We do not know that for certain," the Marquis said, as if he resented being thwarted in his original plan. "We will therefore visit my other Orphanage, which is on the south side of the Estate."

It took them a long time to drive to where the land seemed more thinly populated and the villages through which they passed were smaller.

"I cannot remember ever having been here before," Peregrine remarked.

"We have hunted here," the Marquis replied, "but the woods do not give as much sport as those nearer the Abbey. I do not think we have ever shot here."

"You own too much, Linden," Peregrine said with a sigh. "I am sure it is impossible for you to keep track of everything that goes on on this Estate and on your others."

The Marquis laughed.

"I have Agents and Managers to look after things for me, and so far there are no complaints."

Peregrine thought that if there were any, the Marquis would not be likely to hear of them.

He spent a great deal of his time in London, and when he came to the Abbey it was usually with a large party of amusing people to keep him from being bored.

It was difficult, Peregrine thought a little enviously, to imagine how anyone in the Marquis's position should ever be bored when he was rich enough to have everything he wanted.

There was not a beautiful woman in London who would not be only too willing to take Isobel Sidley's place, now that he had finished with her.

"The trouble with you, Linden," he said aloud, "is that you are too good-looking, too rich, and too successful!"

The Marquis laughed.

"Whatever I have done to provoke that outburst, I certainly do not intend to dispute it."

"You are growing more conceited than Branscombel" Peregrine exclaimed.

"If you say that again," the Marquis replied, "I shall set you down here in the middle of nowhere and make you walk home."

"I thought that would annoy you!" Peregrine chuckled.

The Marquis was just about to make some retort when the Orphanage came in sight.

It was a long, low building, set back from the road on the outskirts of a hamlet consisting of a few cottages, a village green, and a black and white Inn.

The Marquis drew up his horses with a flourish, and as the groom ran to the horses' heads, he fastened the reins to the back-board before he and Peregrine stepped down.

It struck the latter as they walked up to the door that it needed painting, and when he lifted the knocker he noticed that was dirty.

"We will not stay long," the Marquis said, "and if we are not successful here we shall have to think of some other way of finding the girl we require."

"You are not going to be lucky here," Peregrine warned him. "It looks as if no-one is at home."

He raised the knocker again, making a rat-tat that certainly sounded noisy outside the house.

"I am sure if the place is empty I should have been informed," the Marquis said vaguely.

Then they heard footsteps on the other side of the door and a moment later it opened.

The girl who stood there was an unprepossessing sight.

She was wearing an apron of sacking that had holes in it, a dress that, although clean, was threadbare, and her hair, scraped back from her forehead, fell in lank wisps over her ears.

She looked ill and emaciated and the bones of her cheeks seemed unnaturally sharp as she stared first at the Marquis, then at Peregrine, with an expression of surprise on her face.

Then with an obvious start, as if she remembered her manners, she dropped a curtsey.

"I am the Marquis of Alchester," the Marquis

said. "I wish to see over the Orphanage. Is Matron here?"

"Y-yes . . . My Lord."

The question obviously agitated the thin girl.

She spoke with a cultured voice and opened the door a little wider for them to pass through into the Hall. It was bare of furniture and at the end of it was a staircase on which, Peregrine noticed, a number of the bannisters were broken or missing.

The girl moved towards a door.

"P-perhaps . . . Your Lordships . . . should . . . come in here," she said in a voice that seemed to tremble.

As she spoke there was a scream from upstairs. It was the scream of a child in pain, and it was followed by another, and yet another—screams which seemed to echo and re-echo round the empty Hall.

"What is happening?" the Marquis asked sharply. "Has there been an accident?"

"N-no . . . it is . . . Matron."

"Matron?" the Marquis enquired. "What is she doing? Why are those children screaming like that?"

It was difficult to make himself heard above the noise.

Now the girl, who had been gazing upwards, said:

"I must . . . stop her! She will . . . kill little Daisy if she goes on like . . . this!"

She did not wait to say any more, but started to run up the uncarpeted stairs as quickly as she could, and after a moment's hesitation the Marquis and Peregrine followed her.

They reached the landing and saw the girl ahead of them hurry down a short passage which obviously led to a room at the back of the house.

The screams were coming from there, and as they followed the girl through the open door they saw her run towards a woman at the far end of the room who was hitting the children round her with a heavy stick.

She was holding one, a small child of about five

or six, and as the others, trapped between her and a number of beds, were trying to escape she was striking at them too.

They were all screaming and one was lying on the floor with blood pouring from a weal on her back where a blow from the stick had broken the skin.

"Stop, Mrs. Moore! Stop!" the girl cried.

She rushed down the room just as the Marquis and Peregrine entered it, and, seizing the woman's arm, she tried to force it upwards to prevent her from striking again the child she was holding with her other hand.

"Don't you interfere with me!" Mrs. Moore shouted furiously. "These little varmints has woken me again after I told them to be quiet. I'll teach them to obey me orders. I'll beat them until they're unconscious!"

"No, Mrs. Moore! You cannot do that! And you cannot . . . hit Daisy again. She is too . . . ill."

The woman was just about to scream abuse at the girl when she caught sight of the Marquis and Peregrine standing in the doorway.

Her jaw dropped open and she lapsed into silence so that the girl was able to pull the stick from her hand.

Mrs. Moore found her voice.

"Who's this?" she asked.

"H-His . . . Lordship . . . the Marquis!" the girl answered.

Dropping the stick down by one of the beds, the girl put her arm round the small child on whom Mrs. Moore had now relinquished her hold and who was sobbing convulsively.

"It is all right, dearest," she said. "It is all right. She will not hurt you any more."

The other children had already stopped screaming at the sight of the Marquis, and, with the tears running down their thin cheeks, they merely stared at him as if he were an apparition from another world.

The room was a dormitory containing a number of iron bedsteads, most of which were broken and tied up with rope or wire.

The blankets on them were torn and stained, and the pillows appeared to be nothing but bundles of rags.

The Marquis, however, looked at Mrs. Moore as she walked towards him, and he realised from the unsteadiness of her gait and the heightened colour in her florid face that she had been drinking.

She was a largely built, voluptuous creature, dressed in a manner which was a complete contrast to the orphans who were in her charge.

They were in rags, as was the girl who had opened the door, but Mrs. Moore was elegantly attired in a gown that would have been more suitable for a Lady than a working Matron.

There were rings in her ears and on the fingers of her fat hands.

"Your Lordship—this's a shurprishe!" she said, slurring the last word.

She attempted to curtsey and almost fell over in the effort.

"Are you the Matron?" the Marquis asked sharply.

"Yes, indeed, Your Lordship," the woman replied ingratiatingly, "and if you'll come to my Sitting-Room I'll tell you about the difficulties I have here."

The Marquis was looking round the dormitory and at the now-silent, tattered children.

The girl who had let him in was kneeling beside the child lying on the floor, attempting to wipe away the blood from her back.

"Why is this place in such a state?" he asked harshly.

"It's the children. Horrible little varmints they be! Like animals, destroying everything they touch."

Mrs. Moore was obviously now on the defensive, and her dilated eyes and slobbering lips made the Marquis feel physically sick.

He walked away from her towards the girl who was kneeling on the floor.

"It is true that the children are out of control?" he asked.

The girl looked up at him and to his surprise he

saw that there was an undoubted look of hostility in her face.

"If they make a noise," she answered, "and commit the crime of waking Matron, it is because they are hungry."

There was an unmistakable note of condemnation in her voice, and for a moment the Marquis felt she blamed him for what they were suffering.

Then as he looked at the children he realised that what she had said was the truth.

Of course they were hungry. He could see it in the hollowness of their eyes, the way their cheekbones protruded, and the pallor of their skin.

He saw too that the wrist-bones of the girl as she staunched the blood on the child's back were unnaturally sharp.

"Why are they not given enough food?" he asked, and his voice was angry.

He saw that the girl was about to tell him the truth, but even as her lips moved she looked towards the Matron and was afraid to speak.

It was then Mrs. Moore gave a cry that was almost as poignant as that of the children.

"Don't you listen to her, M'Lord! Don't you listen to a word she says!" she screamed. "She's a liar, and she encourages the children in their wickedness!"

"That's enough!" the Marquis said sharply.

At his voice of command, the words Mrs. Moore had been about to speak died in her throat.

"As I can see you are incompetent to run this Orphanage, which bears my name," the Marquis said, "you will leave immediately—within ten minutes. I have no wish to hear anything you have to say, and I will take care that you do not ever have such a post as this again."

Mrs. Moore gave a scream, but the Marquis merely pointed towards the door.

"Go!" he said.

It would have been a brave person who could have argued with him.

However, the Marquis turned away from the Matron and back to the girl on the floor to ask:

"Is there no food in the house?"

She shook her head.

"She spends the money on drink and her own clothes."

The Marquis was about to ask her other questions but instead he said:

"Where can we get some food immediately?"

"You mean you will . . . send out for . . . some?"

"My man will procure anything that is obtainable here and I will send more from the Abbey when I return home."

The girl rose to her feet and carried the child she was holding in her arms to one of the beds. She laid her down and covered her with a torn blanket. Then as the child whimpered and tried to cling to her, she said to one of the older girls:

"Look after Daisy while I tell His Lordship where to buy us some food."

The word "food" seemed to galvanise the silent children into speech.

"Oi'm hungry!" one of the boys shouted.

Then they were all clamouring at once:

"We're hungry! We're hungry!"

For a moment there was an uproar, then the Marquis said firmly:

"Listen to me!" As their voices died away he went on: "I'm going to get you some food immediately, and after this you will be properly fed, but meanwhile you will have to wait and be patient until I can find out what is obtainable. Do you understand?"

It seemed as if they did, and they looked at him with unnaturally large eyes which made him think of small animals which had been ill-treated and did not understand why.

The girl was standing beside him.

"Now, how do I start?" he asked.

"There is a shop that sells . . . bread," she said breathlessly, "and there will be . . . milk at the . . . farm."

"You had better tell me exactly where it is."

"You mean . . . you will . . . fetch it?"

"There does not appear to be anybody else available," the Marquis replied.

"No, there is no-one."

"Explain to me where these places are."

As he spoke, he thought a bread-shop would not be hard to find in such a small village.

"Perhaps ... the farmer's wife will have a ... ham at the farm," the girl suggested as if she had suddenly thought of it, "unless ... it would be too expensive."

The Marquis frowned.

"You must be aware that I am not considering the expense. I wish you to tell me who is responsible for the condition of this place."

He saw by the expression in her eyes that she was well aware who it was.

"Tell me!" he said sharply.

"Please ... let us eat ... first," she begged. "The children have had nothing ... today and very little ... yesterday."

"Very well," the Marquis agreed. "Come downstairs and explain where I should go."

He started to walk towards the stairs as he spoke, followed by Peregrine and the girl. As they reached the Hall he said:

"I suggest, Peregrine, you stay here and see that that ghastly woman leaves without making any further contact with the children. I will not be longer than I can help."

"I have a better idea," Peregrine replied. "I will go and buy what is necessary and you find out the reason for this story state of affairs. After all, it is your Orphanage."

There was a faint twinkle of amusement in the Marquis's eyes, as if he realised that Peregrine had no wish to be left in an uncomfortable position with the drunken Matron.

"Very well," he agreed.

He opened the front door, and as Peregrine got into the Phaeton and picked up the reins, the Marquis said to his groom:

"Help Mr. Wallingham, Jason. You are to buy everything that is obtainable in the village for a large number of hungry children. It does not matter what you get as long as it is food. Do you understand?"

"Yes, M'Lord."

"P-please . . ." a small voice said beside the Marquis, "get the smaller children plenty of milk . . . if they eat too much after being hungry for so long, they will be sick. The farm is just past the Green Man Inn. You cannot miss it."

"I'll find it, Miss," Jason said.

"You had better pay your way, Jason."

The Marquis drew a net purse from his pocket and held it out to the groom.

"I expect they'd give you credit, M'Lord," Jason said with a smile.

It was an impertinence, but the Marquis let it pass.

"Hurry!" he said firmly. "The children will be counting the minutes until you return and so shall I."

Jason took the purse, touched his forehead, and scrambled up onto the Phaeton as Peregrine moved off.

The Marquis turned back to the house.

"I want to talk to you," he said to the girl. "There are a number of questions I have to ask."

The girl seemed to hesitate. Then she opened the door of a room which was very different from those the Marquis had seen so far.

The Marquis realised it was the Matron's Sitting-Room. It was small and comfortable, with a sofa and arm-chairs set in front of a blazing fire.

But much more significant was a table on which there were a number of bottles and a glass from which somebody had recently been drinking.

"She will be in her bedroom, packing, My Lord," the girl said.

The Marquis stood with his back to the fire.

As if she suddenly realised how ragged and dilapidated she looked in contrast to his elegance, the girl undid the sacking-apron and, folding it, set it down on a chair.

The dress she was wearing looked hardly better than the apron. It was worn until the material itself had given way, and so although darned the darns did not hold.

Unnaturally thin though she was, the dress was still too tight and was strained across her thin chest. Because it was too short, the Marquis was aware that she had grown out of it.

"Let me start by asking your name," he said.

"It is . . . Kistna, My Lord."

"Kistna?" he questioned.

"I was born in India."

"How long have you been here?"

"For three years."

The way she spoke told him it had been a long time.

"And your age?"

"I am . . . eighteen, My Lord."

He was just about to ask her why, being so old, she was still in the Orphanage, and as if she knew what she was thinking she explained:

"When my father and mother died of cholera, I was sent here by the Missionary Society with my sister who was only eight."

"She is still here?" the Marquis enquired.

"She . . . died a year ago . . . from the cold in the winter . . . and . . . lack of food."

Now there was no doubt that the note of condemnation was back in Kistna's voice.

"How long has Mrs. Moore been here?" the Marquis asked.

"Nearly two years. There was a kindly Matron here before, but Your Lordship's Agent, Mr. Harboard, retired her as being too old."

"And was she?"

"Not really . . . but I think he wanted to put . . . Mrs. Moore in the position because . . . she was prepared to help him in the . . . way he . . . wished her to . . . do."

The Marquis noted that as she spoke the last sentence Kistna's voice dropped to barely a whisper, and having finished speaking she glanced towards the door almost as if she was afraid that Mrs. Moore would come in to contradict what she had said.

"Do not be afraid," he assured her. "There will be no repercussions, I promise you. I intend to see that what has happened here never occurs again."

Kistna clasped her hands together.

"I hoped Your Lordship would say that. I have often thought I should get in touch with you, for I could not believe you would have countenanced—nor would any decent man—the conditions in this terrible place."

"Tell me about it," the Marquis said. "And I suggest, because you look as if you could do with a good meal, that you sit down while we talk."

Kistna gave a little sigh.

"Thank you, My Lord."

She sat down on the edge of the sofa, but the Marquis remained standing and after a moment he said:

"I can hardly believe what I see when I have just come from the other Orphanage I maintain."

"Things were all right when I first came here," Kistna said, "and Mrs. Owen, who looked after us, was kind and very conscientious."

She paused before she went on:

"My sister was not well and was very unhappy without my mother, so Mrs. Owen allowed me to stay and look after her instead of trying to get employment as I intended to do."

She paused and the Marquis prompted:

"And after your sister's death?"

"The new Matron, Mrs. Moore, found me ... useful. She and Mr. Harboard sacked the women who came in to clean and cook, and I ... took their ... place."

"Why did they do that?"

Kistna's eyes flickered. Then, as if she felt he compelled her to tell him the truth, she said:

"They ... thought they could ... save on the wages, as they did not have to ... pay me."

"What you are saying," the Marquis said slowly, "is that the money they should have been spending on the Orphanage was going into their own pockets."

"I do not think Mrs. Moore got a lot of money,"

Kistna said. "Mr. Harboard gave her drink, which she craved, and paid for most of the gowns she wore. He also gave her . . . other presents."

"Why?" the Marquis enquired.

He saw a flush on Kistna's face and as it turned crimson he knew she was too embarrassed to find the right words, and he said quickly:

"I understand. Go on!"

"I used to hear them talking, and I think this was not the only place from which Mr. Harboard was obtaining money."

Again as she spoke she saw the Marquis's expression change, and she said quickly:

"Please . . . forgive me . . . I should not have said that. It is none of my . . . business, and Mr. Harboard is your . . . servant."

"Not for much longer," the Marquis said ominously. "And I have asked you to be frank with me and tell me the truth, Kistna. There is no-one else to explain to me what has been going on here. I promise you it will never occur again."

"Thank you," Kistna said. "It has been terrible . . . like a nightmare . . . to see the children . . . suffering. Three of them . . . died last year from the cold, although Mrs. Moore tried to explain it was of a . . . fever."

She gave a little sob as she said:

"They used to lie awake at night, because they were so hungry, and though I pleaded and pleaded . . . with Mrs. Moore . . . she would not . . . listen."

"As I have already said, this sort of thing must never happen again! Do you think the last Matron—what was her name?—Mrs. Owen?—would come back?"

"I am sure she would if Your Lordship asked her," Kistna said. "She lives in the village and used to come and call, until Matron told her to keep away and forbade me to open the door to her."

"I will persuade her," the Marquis said, "and I suppose she will know where to buy clothes for the children, blankets for the beds, and so on."

"It was . . . terrible last . . . winter," Kistna said almost beneath her breath.

Then as she spoke she gave a little gasp, for the door opened and Mrs. Moore came in.

She was dressed in a bonnet and cape.

She looked first at the Marquis, then at Kistna, with an expression on her face that was an ugly one.

"I can see Your Lordship's listening to a lot of lies about me," she hissed. "Well, I'm leaving, but them bottles is mine and I'm taking them with me."

She went to the table as she spoke, and, picking up the bottles one by one, she put them into a basket she was carrying over her arm.

When the table was bare she turned to Kistna, who was regarding her with frightened eyes, and said:

"I hope, you little sneak, you die as your sister died, and good riddance to you and the rest of 'em! I've had enough of children to last me a lifetime!"

She flounced round at the last word and went out of the room, slamming the door behind her.

The Marquis saw that Kistna was trembling.

"Forget her," he said. "She cannot harm you! You can be thankful I came here today, or this situation might have gone on for years."

"If it had, we would . . . all have been . . . dead," Kistna replied.

Even as she spoke they heard Mrs. Moore's voice rise as she spoke to somebody and a man replied. Kistna jumped to her feet.

"I think your groom must be back, My Lord, and with the food!"

She did not wait for the Marquis's confirmation but ran across the room and pulled open the door.

She was right.

Jason had come into the Hall carrying a huge basket filled with loaves of bread, and Mrs. Moore was just disappearing down the path which led to the road.

"You are back!" Kistna exclaimed unnecessarily. "And you have brought some food!"

"Mountains of it!" Jason replied with a grin. "Wait till you sees what Oi've got in th' Phaeton."

He spoke to Kistna in a familiar tone. Then as he

saw the Marquis in the doorway, he added in a more respectful voice:

"Oi buys everything as was available, M'Lord, as Your Lordship tells me."

"Quite right," the Marquis approved.

As if the word "food" had somehow penetrated through the closed door leading to the dormitory—or rather, as Kistna guessed, the children had crept along the passage and were listening to what was happening below—there was a sudden cry and they all came rushing down the stairs.

Because it was impossible for Kistna or Jason to stop them, they seized the loaves of bread in their hands, pulling them apart and stuffing large pieces into their mouths in an effort to assuage the hunger in their empty stomachs.

The Marquis would have stepped forward to try to restore some order, but as she realised what he was about to do, Kistna shook her head and, picking up two loaves, put them in his arms.

"Let them eat what they can," she said. "Hold these while I go and heat the milk for the small ones."

Before the Marquis could speak or reply that he was not in the habit of holding loaves of bread, she had run out through the front door, and he saw to his amusement that Peregrine was not only controlling the horses but at the same time keeping them from upsetting a large milk-churn.

Kistna was trying to move the milk-churn by the time the Marquis, still carrying the loaves, was beside the Phaeton.

"I suggest, Peregrine," he said in an amused voice, "that you help Kistna with the milk while I control the horses."

"What you are implying is that it is my turn," Peregrine replied.

He handed over the reins, looking with some surprise at the loaves the Marquis held in his arms.

Then he found himself carrying the milk-churn up the path and into the kitchen of the Orphanage.

On reflection it struck both the Earl and Peregrine how efficiently Kistna managed to get the older children to put out plates and cups on the kitchen-table and help her cut the loaves into small pieces and soak them in milk for the youngest of the orphans.

There were six of them, including the little girl with the injured back, and Daisy, who still seemed half-conscious from the beating she had received at the hands of Mrs. Moore.

They were all fed while Peregrine and the Marquis cut up the hams which Jason had produced from the back of the Phaeton, and there was also a cooked chicken, which the farmer's wife had sold them.

Fortunately, a man appeared from the village to take care of the horses, and Jason was invaluable in keeping the older boys from snatching the food from the younger ones.

By the time everything was distributed evenly and the greediest of them were unable to eat any more, the Marquis had gone in search of Mrs. Owen and brought her back in triumph.

She was just the type of woman who he thought should be in charge of children, and she even wept a little as she told the Marquis how upset she had been at the way they had been treated.

She also related that everybody in the village had been scandalised at Mrs. Moore's behaviour but had realised that as she was a very close personal friend of Mr. Harboard, there was nothing they could do.

"You could have written to me," the Marquis suggested.

"I thought of it, M'Lord," Mrs. Owen said simply, "but we knew Mr. Harboard was in charge of the Estate, and with you away so much in London, we thought perhaps you would never get the letter."

The Marquis told himself angrily that never again would he neglect his responsibilities on his Estate or delegate them to people who were not worthy of his trust.

He seemed to remember far back in his child-hood his Nurse saying: "If you want something done properly, do it yourself!" and that, he told himself bitterly, was the truth.

"What I am asking, Mrs. Owen," he said, "is for you to put things right for me and see that the children have everything they need. I assure you that at the moment no expense need be spared in having things exactly as you think they should be."

He felt that in the circumstances no woman could resist such an opportunity, and he was right.

Mrs. Owen drove back with him in his Phaeton, saying she would send for her personal belongings later, and the children, now that they were fed, and looking quite different from what they had before, greeted her with undeniable pleasure.

"Have there been no new children here since I left?" Mrs. Owen enquired of Kistna.

She shook her head.

"I think Mrs. Moore was offered some more," she replied, "but she always said we were full up, which was not true. There are two empty bedrooms."

She gave a little glance at the Marquis as she spoke, which told him, without her elaborating the point, that Mr. Harboard had undoubtedly collected money for children who were not there and for the same reason had not reported that any of them had died.

By the time he and Peregrine were ready to leave he was in a towering rage at the behaviour of his Agent and was determined to sack him as soon as he got back to the Abbey.

He shook hands with Mrs. Owen, promised her that he would send more food as soon as he got home, and was just about to depart when Peregrine drew him to one side.

"Have you not forgotten something, Linden?" he enquired.

"I hope not," the Marquis replied.

He and Mrs. Owen had discussed the children's clothes, the furnishings, and the women who were to come back to clean and cook as they had always done.

He had agreed to the re-employment of the gardeners who, like the other servants, had been sacked by Mr. Harboard so that he could take their wages for himself.

"The reason we came here," Peregrine prompted.

The Marquis looked at him uncomprehendingly and he went on:

"Surely the girl, Kistna, is just what we are looking for?"

For the moment the Marquis was astonished. Then he looked back down the passage and through the open door of the kitchen where he could see Kistna still at the table, trying to coax Daisy to swallow a few mouthfuls of bread and milk.

She had the child on her lap, and as the Marquis watched her, Daisy, too exhausted to eat, hid her face against her shoulder.

Kistna smiled and kissed her hair.

Then, holding the under-nourished child close in her arms as if she were a baby, she came walking down the corridor.

"I am putting Daisy to bed," she explained to the Marquis as she reached him, "and if she is no better in the morning ... do you think we might send for ... the Doctor?"

She spoke a little anxiously, as if it was an unheard-of extravagance.

The Marquis knew without being told that however ill any of the children had been, Mrs. Moore had never allowed a Doctor to be called in.

Their sufferings had meant nothing to her, and if they died it was just more money in her lover's pocket.

"Of course send for the Doctor, and tonight, if it is necessary," he answered.

He saw a sudden light come into Kristina's eyes and realised that because she was so thin, they had sunk into her face.

Then as she gave him a smile and started to walk up the stairs, he realised that Peregrine was waiting for his answer.

"You are right," he said. "She is quick-witted, and if we feed her she may look more prepossessing. We will collect her tomorrow morning."

Chapter Three

"I do not understand," Kistna said.

The Marquis paused as if he was choosing his words before he replied:

"It is quite simple. Because I feel responsible that you have suffered so much these last three years, I intend that you shall become my Ward."

"Your ... Ward?"

He saw that she did not understand exactly what that entailed, and he said slowly:

"It means that I, as your Guardian, will look after you, provide you with clothes, and when you are restored to health and feel you can face it, I will introduce you to Society."

For a moment Kistna stared at him incredulously. Then she said in a voice that trembled:

"D-do you ... really mean ... that?"

"I assure you that when I make a promise I always carry it through," the Marquis replied.

"Then it is the most ... wonderful thing I can possibly ... imagine could ... happen to me," Kistna said, "and I only wish Papa and Mama could thank you. It is ... difficult for me to find the ... right words."

"I do not want to hear them," the Marquis said.

Peregrine, who was listening, felt that he was a little embarrassed.

They had discussed last night what they should say to Kistna and they had agreed that she must be convinced that she was really the Marquis's Ward.

44

"The less acting and pretence there is about the whole plan, the better," he said. "We must not forget that Branscombe in his own way is intelligent."

Peregrine had agreed that the Marquis's idea of making Kistna in actual fact his Ward was a good one.

They had sat up late discussing the whole idea, and Peregrine had wondered what Kistna's reaction would be. He thought now her gratitude was touching.

There had been many things to do after they had left the Orphanage yesterday. First, the Marquis on his arrival back at the Abbey had sent for his Agent and told the man to leave his employment immediately, adding:

"You know as well as I do what are the penalties for theft, and the lightest sentence you would receive would be one of transportation. However, because I do not wish your appalling behaviour to be known to the outside world, I am letting you go free."

He thought there was an expression of hope in the man's eyes, and he added:

"But you will leave with nothing, not even your personal belongings, which have doubtless been purchased with the money you have stolen from me. You will go only with what you stand up in."

"I have to live, M'Lord," the Agent said in a surly tone.

"If you are hungry it will give you some idea of what those wretched children felt when you refused to feed them," the Marquis said sharply. "Now get out! If I ever see you again I will have you arrested!"

When the Agent, white-faced and shaking, had left the Abbey, the Marquis sent for his Housekeeper.

Mrs. Dawes had been at the Abbey for over twenty years. She had a kindly nature but her department of the house was run with a rod of iron.

She came into the Study in her rustling black silk dress, her long silver chatelaine hanging from her waist.

She dropped the Marquis a respectful curtsey and he said:

"Good-evening, Mrs. Dawes. I need your help."

He guessed that by now Jason's story of what had happened at the Orphanage would have reached the upper servants in the Abbey, and he knew by the expression on Mrs. Dawes's face that she was wondering in what way he would expect her to help the orphans.

"You may have learnt," he began, "that the Orphanage in Westbury Village is a disgrace and the conditions I found there must never be repeated."

"It's something that wouldn't have happened, M'Lord, if certain people who shall be nameless had been trustworthy."

"Things are being put right by the previous Matron," the Marquis explained. "But while I was there I found that through a most regrettable error, my Ward, who had come from India, had been sent to the Orphanage rather than to me here at the Abbey."

This was something Mrs. Dawes obviously had not anticipated, and the Marquis was aware that he had aroused her interest.

He had already decided that Kistna should always be known by her Christian name. It would not make the change, when it came to deceiving Branscombe, too difficult.

" 'Tis a terrible thing to have happened, M'Lord."

"It is indeed, and that is why we must make reparation in every way we can, Mrs. Dawes, for the years she has suffered quite unnecessarily."

"What does Your Lordship wish me to do?"

"First thing in the morning I shall send a carriage to London," the Marquis replied, "to bring back a dressmaker who I know will be able to provide the right type of clothing, but she will naturally require Miss Kistna's measurements."

Mrs. Dawes nodded but did not speak, and the Marquis went on:

"One difficulty, Mrs. Dawes, is that Miss Kistna is actually in rags, and I have no wish for the story of her neglect to be known outside these four walls."

"Of course not, M'Lord!" Mrs. Dawes agreed in a shocked voice.

"You must therefore find her something to wear in which she can receive the dressmaker, and I also require, Mrs. Dawes, a cloak and a bonnet in which to convey her from the Orphanage to the Abbey."

"I understand, M'Lord," Mrs. Dawes said, "and it should not be too difficult. Your Lordship's guests have often left behind gowns for which they had no further use, and which I have kept in case they should come in useful. Mrs. Barnes, the sewing-woman, is at the moment in the Abbey and can alter anything as soon as the young lady arrives."

"Thank you, Mrs. Dawes," the Marquis said.

When the following morning he and Peregrine set off for the Orphanage, he saw that one of the servants had placed a small trunk and a hat-box at the back of the Phaeton.

He was therefore prepared that Kistna should look a little different when they drove back to the Abbey, after there had been a touching farewell to the rest of the children.

They too, the Marquis thought, already looked different. They were cleaner and seemed to be better clothed, and he gathered that they had been provided with garments by the villagers until Mrs. Owen could buy exactly what was required from the nearest town.

One child told him with pride that they had had eggs and bacon for breakfast and another added that there had been honey and hot milk.

They spoke as if, as Peregrine said jokingly, it had been "manna from Heaven."

The Marquis noticed as he drove away with Kistna towards the Abbey that she was very silent, and he guessed it was because she felt that everything that was happening was like being in a dream and she was half-afraid that if she spoke she would wake up.

Now, looking at her in the gown provided by Mrs. Dawes, into which she had changed before she came down to luncheon, he thought that because she was so thin she was ugly, almost to the extent of being grotesque. But that was no reason to assume that with good food and freedom from worry she might not become passable in appearance.

He appreciated that the gown she was wearing was too old for her, and although the seamstress had obviously taken large tucks in at the waist it was still far too big.

But at least she was decently covered, although the bones protruding at her wrists, the hollow shadows around her eyes, and the sharp lines to her chin and cheek-bones were all too obvious.

She was like a very young bird without its feathers, the Marquis thought, and if she looked as she did now when the Earl saw her, he would refuse to marry her, however rich he might think her to be.

Then he consoled himself with the thought that good clothes could make a difference to any woman, and he had always been told that starvation was extremely disfiguring.

Now as he saw the tears of gratitude come into Kistna's eyes he felt uncomfortably that he was being a hypocrite in evoking such a response for something he was doing entirely for his own ends.

Then he pacified his conscience by reflecting that there was hardly a woman in the length and breadth of the country who would not be only too eager to marry the Earl and occupy a position in the Social World that was second to none.

"It is a very great . . . honour that I should be your . . . Ward," Kistna was saying, "but . . . suppose I disappoint you and you become . . . sorry that you did not leave me to earn my own living . . . as I intended to do when I first came to England?"

"At fifteen?" the Marquis enquired.

"I thought . . . perhaps I could be . . . apprenticed to a . . . dressmaking-shop."

The Marquis remembered that he had heard that apprentices had a very hard time. In fact, many of them received such meagre wages that they were as hungry as Kistna had been in the Orphanage.

Aloud he said:

"I think you will find that being my Ward is far more comfortable and definitely more enjoyable."

"But of course," Kistna agreed. "It is only that . . . I am a little afraid."

She looked round the room as if she was realising for the first time how large and luxurious it was.

Then she said in a small voice:

"Papa and Mama were very . . . poor because they were . . . Missionaries, and I am afraid I shall make many . . . mistakes because . . . the way you live is . . . very grand."

The Marquis, however, had already noticed that at luncheon Kistna had watched which cutlery he and Peregrine used and did not pick up a knife or a fork until they had set her an example.

He thought it was intelligent of her and he saw too that she ate delicately, and from the educated way she spoke it was obvious that her parents had been gentlefolk.

"What I am suggesting," he said, "is that until you feel well and have put on a little weight, and have all the clothes with which I intend to provide you, we stay here quietly at the Abbey so that no-one sees you."

"I cannot imagine any . . . place that could be more . . . beautiful!" Kistna exclaimed.

"That is what I hoped you would think," the Marquis replied, "and Mr. Wallingham and I will instruct you about the etiquette you will have to know when I take you to London."

He knew as he spoke that Peregrine looked at him a little questioningly.

They had not really discussed any details of how they should produce the Marquis's Ward, and Peregrine had in fact thought it would be wiser for the Earl to hear that she was at the Abbey and invite himself to stay.

Then he suspected that the Marquis was deliberately making Kistna realise how hard she must work if she was to be a success in the Social World with its Balls and Receptions and endless other forms of entertainment.

Watching Kistna while the Marquis talked to her, he thought she was exceptionally sensitive, and her emotions seemed to mirror themselves in her eyes.

Like the Marquis, he wondered what she would

look like when she was not so pitiably thin and emaciated.

Then the Marquis said:

"I expect Mrs. Dawes has told you that later this afternoon the dressmaker will be arriving from London with a number of gowns that you can wear immediately, and she will make you many more. Do you think it would be wise to rest until she arrives?"

"Yes ... I will do that," Kistna said obediently, "but please ... My Lord ... would it be ... possible for me to have some books to ... read? There are many in the Library."

"You like reading?" the Marquis enquired.

"It has been agonising these past three years when there was nothing I could read in the Orphanage except for my Bible."

She gave a shy little smile as she said:

"It is now the only possession I own, because all the other things that came with me from India have either fallen to bits or I have given them to the children."

As she spoke, the Marquis knew that she would have given the children who were suffering from hunger and cold all the warm clothing she owned.

Because he thought it was a mistake for her to go on thinking about the past, he said:

"There is a large selection of books in the Abbey, and you must get my Curator to show you the shelves on which you will find the latest novels, including those of Sir Walter Scott."

"There is so much I want to read," Kistna said in a rapt voice.

Then there were tears both in her eyes and in her voice as she said to the Marquis:

"Is this true? Really ... true that I am here and will be your Ward? To live in this ... wonderful ... magnificent house?"

"It is true."

"How can I thank you ... except by asking ... God to do that for me."

"You have thanked me," the Marquis said firmly.

"Too many protestations of gratitude will make me embarrassed, so I would prefer it, Kistna, if you give me your thanks in actions, and not in words."

"How can I . . . do that?"

"By doing exactly what I tell you, and by putting some flesh on your bones as quickly as possible."

Kistna gave a little laugh.

"That is exactly what Mrs. Dawes said to me, and she has already made me drink two huge glasses of milk since I arrived!"

"You will find that Mrs. Dawes invariably knows best," the Marquis said, "and as I also like having my own way, you must do exactly what we tell you."

"You know I want to . . . please you," Kistna said simply.

When she left them the Marquis turned to Peregrine with a smile on his face.

"What do you think of our *protégée* so far?" he enquired.

"She is definitely intelligent," Peregrine said. "I am just wondering how long it will be before she puts, as you said, some flesh on her bones."

"Clothes will make a difference and will give her confidence."

"I know you are an expert on what clothes mean to a woman," Peregrine teased, "but I think where Kistna is concerned it will not be only her looks that count but her character."

The Marquis held up his hand in protest.

"Oh, for Heaven's sake!" he ejaculated. "The last thing we want is a girl with character! What we require is a nice, complacent creature who will do exactly what we tell her and accept the idea of marrying Branscombe as being a gift from Heaven itself!"

Peregrine was silent for a moment. Then he said:

"I think Kistna is different from the average girl. She has lived in India with her father and mother, and she has certainly suffered in England. I doubt if she will ever be the fat, complacent cow that you are imagining in the part you wish her to play."

"Very well then," the Marquis said, as if he must defend himself. "She is intelligent, and therefore when we get to the point of telling her exactly what she has to do, that she has to pretend to be Mirabelle, she will see at once that it is very much to her advantage. Even being Branscombe's wife is preferable to starving to death in an Orphanage."

"I am sure if she gives her mind to it she will be admirable in the part," Peregrine replied. "I am only wondering if she will have an opinion in the matter."

"If she has an opinion it will be to thank her lucky stars that she will live in extreme comfort for the rest of her life and that, if Branscombe is angry at being deceived, there will be nothing he can do about it."

The Marquis spoke sharply. Peregrine decided that there was no point in continuing the conversation and suggested that they go riding.

When they returned several hours later, it was to find that the dressmaker had arrived and was waiting to see the Marquis.

She was a sharp-faced, clever woman who had made her business one of the most successful in Bond Street.

The Marquis had in the past accompanied a number of his mistresses and his social *chère amies* to Madame Yvonne's dress-shop.

She was known to be discreet and she never made the mistake of letting the woman the Marquis was providing with an expensive gown be aware that she had served him on other occasions.

Now she dropped him a curtsey and waited politely for him to give her his orders.

"I want you, Madame, to dress my Ward in the very latest creations," he said, "and provide her with a wardrobe which will excel that of every other debutante in Society."

Madame Yvonne could not conceal the glint of excitement in her eyes, but she replied in a quiet tone:

"I will, as usual, do my very best to please Your Lordship."

"There is one condition attached to this order."

"Yes, My Lord?"

"It is that for the moment I do not wish anyone in London to know that my Ward is here with me at the Abbey."

He saw the surprise in Madame Yvonne's expression, and went on:

"You will understand when I explain that Miss Kistna has been ill, and nothing could be more of a handicap for a young girl than to be thought to have ill-health or to suffer from temporary or permanent ailments, whatever they may be."

Madame Yvonne nodded her agreement and the Marquis continued:

"That is why, Madame, I have no intention of allowing anyone to know that my Ward is here, until she is well enough to grace your gowns and the Ball-Rooms where she will appear in them."

"Of course, I understand, My Lord," Madame Yvonne said, "and I promise that not a word about the young lady will pass my lips."

"Thank you," the Marquis said. "And now make sure that everything which you provide is of the finest and best quality."

He paused before he added:

"My Ward is a great heiress and there is no need to cheesepare in any manner."

As he spoke he knew this meant he would doubtless be overcharged on a great number of items on the bill.

At the same time, he had planted the idea in Madame Yvonne's mind that Kistna was an heiress, and he suspected that later she would not be able to prevent herself from dropping a hint to those in the Social World that his Ward was very rich.

It all fitted in like a puzzle to the general plan, the Marquis thought, and congratulated himself on his eye for detail.

He decided to tell Mrs. Dawes that quite a num-

ber of gowns would be left for Kistna today, and
others would be arriving almost daily as soon as they
were ready.

"What does Miss Kistna feel about her new
clothes?" the Marquis asked.

"I've never seen a young lady so excited or so
thrilled with the gowns which Madame Yvonne
brought her," Mrs. Dawes replied. "In fact, now that
the excitement's over I've put her to bed, and I'll be
exceedingly surprised if she's not fast asleep, M'Lord,
and sleeping like a child, from sheer exhaustion!"

"I knew I could leave her in your capable hands,
Mrs. Dawes," the Marquis said, and the Housekeeper
was delighted with the compliment.

He did not see Kistna again until she came down
to dinner that evening, when she certainly looked very
different from the ragged orphan he had first met.

As she was so pale and obviously anaemic from
lack of food, Madame Yvonne had not dressed her
immediately in the traditional white of a débutante.

Her gown was of soft periwinkle blue, and its full
skirt and large balloon-like sleeves concealed the skel-
eton-like slimness of her figure.

There was little that could be done about her
face except to add a little rouge to her cheeks.

But either Mrs. Dawes or one of the housemaids
had concealed Kistna's lank hair with skilfully arranged bows of satin ribbon which matched her
gown.

There was a narrow band of velvet of the same
colour to encircle her long neck.

She came into the Salon a little shyly, where the
Marquis and Peregrine were waiting, and as she
walked towards them they both saw that the Marquis
had been right in thinking that clothes could change a
woman.

He felt that because she was so thin and therefore very light, Kistna walked with a special grace
that reminded him in a strangely poetical manner of a
flower moving in the breeze.

When she smiled at him he saw that Madame
Yvonne had advised her to wear a little lip-salve,

which certainly prevented her lips from looking so pale and bloodless.

"Fine feathers make fine birds!" Peregrine said, before the Marquis could speak.

"That is what I ... hoped you would ... say," Kistna replied with a little laugh, "and I do indeed feel like a peacock spreading my tail in this beautiful gown."

She glanced at the Marquis and said in a low voice almost as if she spoke to him alone:

"I want ... to ... thank you ..."

"I have told you, I dislike being thanked."

As he spoke, he thought he had never in his whole life seen such an expression of overwhelming gratitude in a woman's eyes.

He remembered how offhand Lady Isobel had been about a diamond necklace she had wanted for Christmas, and when he had given it to her she had complained that he had omitted to purchase the bracelet that went with it.

He remembered too other jewels he had given to attractive Cyprians whom he had installed in one of his houses in Chelsea in the manner that was expected by their profession.

They had extorted everything they could from him, and, as Peregrine had said: "had a magnet which drew the gold coins out of his pockets." But their gratitude had always sounded contrived.

It struck the Marquis as rather touching that this girl had such a joyous delight in being well dressed, and as he met her eyes he found himself thinking it was a pity, in a way, that there had to be an ulterior motive for giving her the clothes.

Then he told himself that this was not the moment for becoming sentimental. Besides, they had a long way to go before he was ready to cheat the Earl as he had been cheated.

Merely to think of it made the Marquis scowl, although he had no idea that he was doing so, until Kistna said in a frightened little voice:

"You are ... angry? Is it ... something I have ... said or ... done?"

"No, of course not!" the Marquis replied. "And I hope never to be angry with you or to make you afraid that I might be."

"I should be very . . . very afraid if you were . . . angry with me."

"You would have reason to be," Peregrine interposed, "for I assure you the Marquis can be very overpowering when he is in a rage, and what makes it worse is that he never raises his voice."

Kistna gave a nervous little laugh.

"I agree . . . that is much worse than someone . . . who shouts."

She paused before she went on:

"Papa was never angry if someone did anything wrong. He was only hurt and upset and that made one penitent immediately."

"How do you behave when you are angry?" Peregrine asked.

"Sometimes I lose my temper," Kistna admitted, "but it is over quickly, and then I am sorry . . . very, very sorry . . . and want to apologise."

"That is the right and generous way to behave," Peregrine approved.

"I am sure I could never be angry in such beautiful surroundings as these," Kistna said. "There are two things that make people angry—ugliness and injustice."

"Particularly injustice," the Marquis said in a hard voice.

Once again he was thinking of the Earl, and, as if Peregrine thought it was a mistake for his mind to dwell on his enemy, he quickly changed the subject and when they walked into dinner all three were laughing.

To Kistna it was a fascination that she had never known before, not only to dine in such luxurious surroundings but to eat food that she thought must taste like the ambrosia of the gods.

It was also an enchantment she found hard to express to be alone with two such distinguished, elegant, delightful men.

Thinking back into the past, she knew her father had always seemed rather serious, although he laughed when they were together as a family and there was a warmth and love in everything they said to each other.

But it was not the same as listening to two Gentlemen of Fashion who exchanged witticisms almost as if they duelled with each other not with swords but with words, and every cut and thrust of their tongues had a subtle meaning.

Because Kistna felt that over the last three years she had been starved not only of food for her body but of food for her brain, she found every moment that she listened to the Marquis and his friend as stimulating as any lesson she might have been given by the most experienced teacher.

Because she was no longer hungry, she could appreciate the subtlety of a word, of a turn of phrase, and could concentrate on the Marquis and his friend without her mind slipping away as it would have done a few days ago.

Sometimes they talked to her, but more often they appeared to forget that she was with them.

They discussed sport or their acquaintances with the freedom of two men who are so close to each other that much of what they said had no need for elaboration.

Peregrine talked to the Marquis of his chances of winning the Gold Cup at Ascot. Then he said, as if he suddenly remembered Kistna's presence:

"Are you fond of horses?"

"I love them!" Kistna replied. "But I have never had a chance of riding the sort of horses you are talking about. All we could afford in India were the small-boned little animals, which were very spirited and often bolted in a manner which was almost impossible to control."

The Marquis smiled.

"Do I understand that you are longing to ride one of my horses?"

Kistna gave a little cry.

"Please . . . please . . . could I have a habit? Then perhaps you would . . . allow me to ride with you and Mr. Wallingham."

"I have ordered you two habits, as it happens," the Marquis replied, "and they are what you will need for the summer. You will require something warmer when winter comes."

Instead of thanking him, he saw that Kistna was staring at him with a look of bewilderment.

"What is it?" he asked.

"I cannot understand how you can know . . . exactly what a woman needs. Madame Yvonne was saying today that you have such excellent taste, and I wonder how, as you are unmarried, you have learnt about gowns, bonnets, and even habits?"

There was a pause as the Marquis wondered how he should reply to such an artless question.

He was well aware that Peregrine's eyes were twinkling and that he had been as surprised by it as he was himself.

Kistna was waiting for his answer and after a moment he said:

"I may be a bachelor, but I have a large number of female relatives."

"Oh . . . of course! I never thought of that!" she exclaimed. "Mrs. Dawes told me that your mother was very, very beautiful, and I expect she taught you about how much clothes mean to a woman, especially someone like me . . . who has never had any."

The Marquis glanced across the table at Peregrine and, without speaking, dared him ever to tease him about this conversation.

Then, as if she sensed what they were thinking, Kistna looked from one to the other and asked:

"H-have I said . . . something wrong? Was it . . . incorrect of me to . . . question His Lordship's knowledge of what . . . pleases a lady?"

"No, of course not!" Peregrine said reassuringly. "When you know the Marquis better, you will find he is extremely knowledgeable on every subject, whether it appertains to women or to horses."

"There is so much I want to learn about horses," Kistna cried, and the awkward moment passed.

After dinner the Marquis and Peregrine played piquet, gambling fiercely against each other and betting large sums on each game.

Kistna watched them for a little while, then she moved down the Salon, looking at the objets d'art, which were extremely valuable, and the paintings, each of which held her attention for a long time.

The game finished and the Marquis walked across the room to stand beside her.

He found she was looking at a very beautiful Poussin where nymphs gambolled in the foreground against a forest glade and misty mountains.

"Do you like that painting?" he enquired.

"It is ... difficult to put into words ... what I feel about it," Kistna said in a rapt little voice.

The Marquis was interested.

"I would like you to tell me, however difficult it may be, what you feel."

She did not answer for a moment, then she said:

"When we were in India there were many strange carvings on the Temples which shocked the English, and they complained to Papa."

"What did your father do about them?"

"I asked him what he was going to do," Kistna said, "and he told me that he tried to understand why the Indians had carved such erotic figures on what to them was a place of sanctity."

She looked up at the Marquis to see if he was listening, and went on:

"Papa said that each Indian craftsman used the life-force within himself to create through his fingers something that to him expressed his faith and his belief."

She paused and again looked at the Marquis, this time a little appealingly.

"I am not explaining it well," she said, "but I think Papa was trying to say that each man who creates anything to which he gives his heart is like God and is, in his own way, a creator."

"I have never heard that theory before," the Marquis said.

"You asked me what I felt about this painting," Kistna went on, "and I feel that Nicholas Poussin poured his own life-force into it, and it is therefore a creation not so much of his mind as of his soul and his heart."

The Marquis stared at her in sheer astonishment.

It seemed to him incredible that this girl, whom he still thought of as an inmate of the Orphanage, could not only think so profoundly but could express herself so ably in a way that he might himself have found very difficult.

"Do all paintings make you feel like that?" he enquired.

"I have never seen one like this before," she said, "nor like any of the others here in this room. But India is full of paintings and India itself is sheer beauty."

"You speak as if you miss it."

"I miss the happiness I knew there," Kistna said, "and because it is the only beautiful thing I have had to think of these last few years, it is very vivid in my mind and very real."

The Marquis could understand that the only way in which she could escape from the horror of her surroundings was through her imagination and her memories of the past.

Because she made him feel sentimental, he said sharply:

"Now that you have beautiful things in the present, you must think of them and, because you are young, of the future. That is what matters—what lies ahead."

"Yes . . . of course," Kistna agreed. "But it is only today being here with you that I have felt for the first time that I have a future. Before, it was only a matter of time before I died as my sister died of the cold and hunger."

She spoke quietly in a voice that was not dramatic in any way, which somehow made it more poignant and more moving.

The Marquis had a strange impulse to put his

arm about her shoulders, hold her against him, and tell her she need never be frightened again.

He knew it was what he would have done to a child, but he remembered that Kistna was not a child but a grown-up young woman who would doubtless misunderstand such an action on his part.

"Now you have a great, positive future, and I think a very exciting one!" he said.

The way he spoke seemed to break the spell that had existed for some moments between him and the girl standing beside him.

* * *

Later that night when Kistna was alone in the darkness of her bed, she found herself thinking of the Marquis's words and the way he had said: "A very exciting future," almost as if he knew what would happen to her.

"What could be more exciting than being here and becoming the Marquis's Ward?" she asked herself.

And yet, perceptively, she knew there was something more; something she felt was in the Marquis's mind ever since she had met him.

She remembered that her mother had often said to her father:

"There is something about India, darling, that makes one intuitive, or is it perceptive?"

"The two are almost synonymous," the Reverend John Lovell had said with a smile.

"Not to me," his wife had replied. "It is difficult to express what I mean, but at times I feel I am closer to the Other World, the world in which both you and I belong, darling, than I am to this world."

"I think perhaps that happens to everybody who comes to India," Kistna's father answered. "It is as if the faith of the people is intensified by the heat and the dryness until one can feel it vibrating everywhere."

"I am sure that is it," Mrs. Lovell said. "The vibrations of your faith, and you, my dearest, make you very real."

They smiled at each other across the table, and Kistna had thought that she could feel the vibrations of their love as clearly as her mother felt the vibrations of faith.

Looking back, she was sure that their house, small though it was, had been filled with the love and happiness that is rich beyond the dreams of avarice.

"We were so happy," she would cry despairingly when she lay in the darkness on the hard bed in the dormitory. "Oh, Mama, Papa, how could you ... die and leave me ... all alone?"

She tried to tell herself that they were near her and to find them she had only to reach out from the confines of the material world.

But somehow, because she was so cold and hungry, it was difficult to link with the unseen or with the love she had lost.

Now she felt as if her mother and father were beside her again, talking to her, guiding her, and she knew that her love for them and theirs for her was as strong as it had ever been.

"I am lucky, so very, very lucky," Kistna told herself.

Perhaps it had been her mother who had guided the Marquis to the Orphanage to save her and the children from a hell which had seemed to stretch endlessly into an empty future.

Now there was tomorrow, the next day, and the day after that, and she would be with the Marquis, who, almost like a Medieval Knight, had destroyed the dragon in the shape of Mrs. Moore.

"He is wonderful, Mama!" Kistna said in her heart. "So wonderful and so handsome! He is very kind to me and has given me all these wonderful clothes. At the same time, there is ... something I do not ... understand."

She thought and tried to put it into words.

"It is something he is thinking about me; something that is not just kindness but something else."

She tried to express it, but the words would not come.

She knew only that behind the Marquis's eyes

there was a mystery she could not solve and that vibrating from him there was something different from what she had expected.

It made her a little afraid.

It made her feel that even in the dream-world into which he had taken her, where she lived in the most fantastically beautiful house she had ever imagined, where she was waited on and dressed as if she were a Princess, there was still something that she found herself questioning, like a note of music that was not quite true.

Then she thought she was being absurd.

"I am lucky ... so very ... very lucky," she said aloud. "Thank You, God, for sending him, and thank You for making him my Guardian."

Chapter Four

"I wonder if we are being missed in London?" Peregrine asked.

"I imagine there is plenty of speculation about our absence," the Marquis replied drily, "especially in certain quarters."

Peregrine knew he was referring to Lady Isobel, and he thought she would not only be bewildered but curious to know why, when there were so many attractive gaieties in London, the Marquis had chosen to retire to the country.

Almost as if their conversation had evoked a response, the Marquis's secretary, Mr. Barnes, came to the door to say:

"There is a letter from London for Your Lordship and a groom has been told he is to wait for an answer."

He held out a note as he spoke, and the Marquis, without taking it from him, saw the flamboyant crest on the back of the envelope and said:

"Send the groom back with a message to say that you are unable to get in touch with me and it would be useless for him to wait for me to return to the Abbey."

Mr. Barnes's expression did not alter. He merely replied: "Very good, My Lord," and left the room.

"Isobel?" Peregrine questioned.

The Marquis nodded.

"She is extremely persistent, but I have no intention of being embroiled with her again. I realise now it was a mistake from the very beginning."

"I could have told you that," Peregrine said, "but I doubt if you would have listened."

The Marquis did not answer, and he went on:

"Even though she is a beauty, I have always thought that at heart Isobel is a bad woman, and that is not something I say about many 'Fair Charmers.'"

Again the Marquis did not respond, and as Peregrine knew he disliked talking about his love-affairs, even to his most intimate friends, he was not surprised.

At the same time, because he was extremely fond of the Marquis he was glad that he had realised in time that Isobel was not only no good but also dangerous.

Because the new situation was uppermost in both their thoughts, Peregrine, having dismissed Isobel, was thinking once again of Kistna.

"Have you noticed how different she looks after only four, or is it five, days of decent food and pretty clothes?" he asked the Marquis.

"She has certainly put on a little weight."

"I have the feeling," Peregrine said, "that by the time we have finished her rehabilitation she will turn out to be a beauty."

"Do you really think so?" the Marquis remarked.

He did not sound particularly interested, and Peregrine replied almost aggressively:

"Where are your eyes, Linden? Personally, I find it fascinating to notice the change which I can see taking place every day, or I could almost say every hour. She is certainly no longer the little scarecrow she was when we first saw her at the Orphanage."

He gave a little laugh.

"Now that I look back, I can think of nothing more fantastic than that moment when we arrived and Kistna, in rags, looking as if she might die at any moment, opened the door."

He saw that the Marquis was listening and continued:

"Then there was all that screaming upstairs and we found that devilish woman beating those wretched children. It was just like something out of a book."

"I will certainly never allow such a thing to happen again on any property of mine," the Marquis said harshly.

"How is Rodwell shaping up?" Peregrine enquired.

"I like him," the Marquis answered, "and as he has always lived on the Estate and knows everything and everybody, he is a far better Agent than the last swine I employed."

"You were wise to take him on," Peregrine agreed. "It is always a mistake, I think, to bring in a stranger."

"I agree, and, as you say, I have been wise in this particular."

"And a great many others as well," Peregrine said with a smile. "Now, to get back to what is the really important question—when are we going to produce Kistna like a rabbit out of a hat and start tricking Branscombe into proposing marriage?"

"She is not yet ready!"

"Personally, I do not think we have far to go."

"What you are really saying is that you are bored with being here and want to get back to London."

"I have said nothing of the sort!" Peregrine objected sharply. "I always enjoy being with you, Linden. And as long as I have superb horses to ride and your wine-cellar at my disposal, I have no complaints."

"What about Molly, or whatever her name was?" the Marquis enquired.

Peregrine grinned.

"I never could really afford her, and being with you here I am not only saving on her board and lodging but on all the things I should undoubtedly have been persuaded into giving her, even though I could not pay for them!"

"I am glad to be of service!" the Marquis remarked.

Peregrine laughed.

"I am enjoying myself and there is no pretence about it! I have the feeling, although I may be wrong, that I can say the same thing about you."

The Marquis did not answer him immediately, and Peregrine was certain that even if he would not admit it, he was not half as bored as he had been before the Derby.

There had been no doubt then that nothing interested him particularly, and, with his liaison with Isobel coming to an end, there was little to look forward to except the familiar round of entertainments and the same crowd of friends and "hangers-on."

There was no doubt, Peregrine thought shrewdly, that Kistna had brought something into his life that had been lacking.

The Marquis in fact was concentrating very seriously on seeing that she acquired all the graces and attributes that were required of a debutante.

"More than that," he said to Peregrine, "Mirabelle is different from most young girls her age."

"In what way?" Peregrine enquired.

"Because she has always been so rich," the Marquis answered, "she has had the best teachers, not only for her education but also for all the other talents a young girl is expected to produce for the 'Marriage Market.'"

Peregrine raised his eye-brows.

"The 'Marriage Market'?" he questioned.

"What else is it?" the Marquis enquired. "Their parents groom them like show-horses and bring them to London to parade them before bachelors like you and me, hoping to captivate our fancy."

He spoke so cynically that Peregrine looked at him in surprise. Then he laughed.

"What else do you expect them to do?" he enquired. "A woman's sole aim in life is to get married."

"And a man's is to avoid it!"

Peregrine thought this over. Then he answered:

"That is not quite true. After all, unless my elder brother has a regrettable accident, it does not matter if I remain a bachelor for the rest of my life, but you have to continue the family and sooner or later produce a son, or rather two or three to be on the safe side!"

"It was drummed into my head almost from the moment I was born that that was my duty towards the family," the Marquis remarked with a note in his voice that told his friend he had always disliked the idea.

"It is strange," Peregrine ruminated, "that you have never fallen in love."

"I have taken damned good care not to get involved in the 'Marriage Market,'" the Marquis said. "In fact, I cannot remember when I last met a girl of Kistna's age, which makes it rather difficult."

"In what way?"

"I am not certain how much she should know, or how ignorant she will appear among other débutantes."

"If you ask me," Peregrine said, "she is so quick-witted that she will make most of them seem like suet-puddings."

"She is still too thin," the Marquis said sharply.

"The curves are there, and that is the important thing," Peregrine said. "I remember my father saying: 'A woman should be curved and a man straight.' He was looking at the Prince Regent's stomach as he spoke."

"Poor old 'Prinny'! He was very ashamed of it," the Marquis smiled, "especially the last years when he used to drive out only in a closed carriage, and when I visited him at Windsor he always kept the blinds half-drawn."

"He ate and drank too much and had done so all his life," Peregrine said. "I do not mind betting, Linden, that you will keep your figure until you reach the grave."

"I certainly hope so," the Marquis replied. "Which reminds me, the horses are waiting and I told Kistna she could come with us."

"I thought that would be the reason why we were not leaving earlier."

"She had to have her French lesson," the Marquis

said. "Incidentally, we were fortunate to find that woman to teach her. Her accent is perfect, but then she is Parisian."

"I have a feeling that by the time you have finished with Kistna she will be stuffed like a Christmas goose. Men hate a clever woman, and if she entered the 'Marriage Market' of which you are so scathing, she will frighten her suitors away rather than attract them."

"With her fortune?" the Marquis asked cynically.

"You have not told her yet that she has to pretend to be Mirabelle?" Peregrine enquired.

"No, of course not!" the Marquis replied. "You know we agreed that we would train her together, and I would not dream of taking such an important step in her development without discussing it with you first."

"I am glad you are being cautious," Peregrine said. "I may be wrong, but I have the feeling she will not like pretending to be another woman."

"I am not concerned with her feelings," the Marquis said in a lofty tone. "She will do as she is told, and personally I anticipate no difficulties of any sort."

"Why not?"

"Because Kistna is so grateful for what I have done for her that I am quite certain she would obey any order I give her, whatever it may be."

Peregrine was about to argue, then changed his mind.

He could not help thinking that the Marquis was over-confident and that women, however young they might be, were invariably unpredictable.

But there was no point in saying so, and he kept silent.

* * *

Kistna, having said good-bye politely to her French mistress, had run on winged feet to her bedroom to change into her riding-habit.

It had been difficult for the last quarter-of-an-hour of the lesson to concentrate on *Mademoiselle's*

voice and not to watch the clock, knowing that by the
time the hands reached eleven she would be free and
could be riding with the Marquis and Mr. Wallingham.

She had never thought her life could change
overnight from misery and despair to a happiness
which seemed to make everything golden and spark-
ling like the sun.

When she looked back to the moment when she
had opened the door to the two most handsome and
elegant gentlemen she had ever seen in her life, how
could she have imagined that they were taking her
from an old world to a new one, where everything
had an unmistakably dream-like quality?

"It cannot be true," she said to herself as she put
on one of the habits which had arrived from London.

'It cannot be true!' she thought as she ran down
the carved gilt staircase to find the Marquis and
Peregrine in the Hall, with three magnificent horses
waiting for them outside.

The Marquis was himself teaching her to ride,
and he was extremely insistent that she hold the reins
in the right way and sit in her saddle like a born
equestrian.

She learnt to take her fences in a manner which
brought her the enthusiastic approval of Peregrine, if
not of the Marquis.

She had learnt, however, to know when he was
pleased by the expression in his eyes. But it was not
only in riding that he was her tutor.

He taught her when she came into a room to
walk at a measured pace, to stop at exactly the right
place, to drop a curtsey, and to carry her head at
precisely the correct angle as she did so.

He made her rehearse it over and over again until
he had obtained the perfection he desired. Then there
were similar instructions for greeting people, for saying good-night, and for proceeding to the Dining-
Room for meals.

"If you ask me, you expect too much," Peregrine
had protested once or twice.

"If she is pretending to be my Ward, I expect her

to be faultless in her behaviour in any and every circumstance," the Marquis answered.

He thought Peregrine looked sceptical, and he added:

"Make no mistake—Branscombe, who is a stickler for etiquette and protocol, will notice the slightest fault, and we have no desire to make him suspicious until the knot is tied."

Peregrine had to agree that this was common sense and certainly Kistna made no complaints.

She appeared to be as anxious as the Marquis was that everything she did should be perfect.

Riding now through the Park and into the fields beyond, Kistna was on a horse that was spirited but well trained and responded to almost everything she required of him.

As they drew in their mounts after a long gallop, she said with a little sigh:

"I never imagined it would be possible to move so fast. Since your horses must be swifter than anyone else's, I am not surprised you win so many races."

"I am certainly hoping to win the Gold Cup at Ascot," the Marquis replied.

"Will I be able to see it?"

The Marquis turned to look at her and she knew this was something he had not considered.

"Please ... let me!" she pleaded. "It would be ... so exciting to see your horse first past the Winning-Post."

"Actually," the Marquis said, "I had not thought of your being there."

He looked at Peregrine and they both realised it would be a mistake for Kistna to be seen at such a fashionable gathering. There might well be someone present who had met Mirabelle in Italy.

She looked from one man to the other and was aware that there was something passing through their minds that she did not understand.

"Am I ... doing something ... wrong?" she enquired.

"No, of course not," the Marquis said. "It is just that I had not considered taking you with us to Ascot and it is something I must think about before I agree."

The way he spoke told Kistna that it would not be an easy decision for him to make, although why there should be any difficulty about it she did not understand.

More than either the Marquis or Peregrine she was aware of the difference in her appearance.

In fact, every day that she was at the Abbey she was becoming more like the girl who had come confidently from India to England, thinking that while it might be different she would soon find a way of looking after herself and eventually her younger sister as well.

Because she had been so happy in her home life, Kistna had never known fear—either of people or of living.

It was only when Mrs. Moore had come to the Orphanage that she found herself trapped in an appalling terror from which she could find no way of escape.

To begin with, she could not leave her sister to try to earn her own living in the world outside.

Then when little Indira died, Kistna had not the will-power or stamina to break away, besides which she had a feeling that Mrs. Moore would not have allowed her to go.

She had thought that all that lay ahead of her was death—a slow, humiliating, agonising death from hunger, cold, and misery because she must watch the children suffering and dying round her.

Then like a miracle everything had changed and it seemed to her as if the Marquis were the Archangel Michael lifting her from the darkness into the light.

It was the light which she had left behind when she had been taken from the warm sunlight of India into the fog, the mist, and the cold that she found in the Orphanage.

At night when she had lain with only a threadbare blanket to keep out the cold, she had tried to imagine the sun beating down on the roof of her father's bungalow.

She had seen the flowers which her mother loved brilliant in the small garden, and had felt the warmth percolating through her starved body, so that she felt as if she were part of the sunshine which turned to gold the river whose name she bore.

Because she had been brought up in a world which was beautiful wherever she looked and wherever she went, it was the ugliness of the Orphanage apart from everything else which seemed to eat into her very soul.

The ugliness of the chilly rooms, the broken beds, the dirty floors, her terror of Mrs. Moore with her face flushed with drink and her voice screaming abuse, and the children with their protruding bones and tattered ragged clothes.

Finally there was the ugliness and pain of hunger; the tears of helplessness and despair.

Kistna would remember how much her father had loved beauty and especially the beauty he had found in India.

It was in fact a desire to discover a new land, one to which his mind and heart had been drawn long before he saw India, which had made the Reverend John Lovell volunteer for Missionary work in a country where the evangelical fervour of reformation had not yet been known.

The gentlemen of the East India Company had not originally intended to govern India but merely to make money there.

This they had done very effectively in the Eighteenth Century, gradually assuming more and more responsibility, until in 1813 the Company's trade monopoly with India was abolished and for the first time public opinion in England began to have some direct effect upon British administration.

The East India Company had hitherto forbidden Christian Missionaries to come to India, but with the Crown appointing a Governor-General and the board from Westminster having ultimate authority, the ban was lifted.

The Reverend John Lovell had learnt the previous year that this would happen, and it was one of his relatives in the East India Company who had suggested to him that here was a country where he would find Missionary work preferable to being an underpaid Curate in England.

"You may not convert many of the heathens," his relative had said, "since the Indians are religious enough in their own way not to want any alien faith. But you will have a good time and it will certainly widen your horizons."

John Lovell had jumped at the chance of going abroad, especially to the East, and while he was considering it there was another reason, a very personal one, which forced him to make up his mind quickly and to leave England towards the end of 1812.

He was therefore first in the field, and when the next year the Company ban on Christian Missionaries was lifted, they swarmed in in their hundreds to look with horror at the wickedness they found in this enormous and strange country.

The savagery, the hideous customs of widow-burning, infanticide, and religious extortion, convinced them that they had to fight a crusade against the devil himself.

But they found what John Lovell had already discovered: the religious faith of the Indians was so deep-seated, an intrinsic part of their very breathing, that Christianity had no appeal, no attractions to offer a people who believed that every sin or virtue in this life was punished or rewarded in the next.

The Reverend John in fact made very little effort to convert those who believed fervently in one set of gods into embracing another faith.

Because he was an extremely intelligent man, he found that the history of India and its different castes fascinated him.

Instead of being a teacher he became a pupil.

It was doubtful if he ever made a convert, but because he was sincere and because the Indians knew they could trust him, he made friends in every sect and caste from the untouchables to the Brahmans, from the lowest sweepers to the Maharajahs.

Therefore, as Kistna grew up she met an amazing variety of Indians and learnt through her father to recognise the differences in their beliefs and creeds, their characters and outlooks.

To the other English whom they met first at Calcutta, and later when they travelled up-country, anyone with coloured skin was a "native." But to the Lovells they were people and each was more fascinating than the last.

In fact, though they did not realise it, John Lovell and his wife were like the first pioneers of the East India Company who had developed a trading policy and had little wish for anything else.

They had no wish in those first years to convert the Sub-continent, which would have seemed a preposterous ambition.

They had treated the native Princes with respect and often affection and had tolerated the religions of the country. Often they were men of aesthetic sensibilities who responded sensuously and appreciatively to the beauty of India.

Kistna could remember her father standing looking at a sunset or across the silver river to the desert beyond, and saying with reverence in his voice:

"Could anything be more beautiful, more a part of God?"

She felt that he found the God in whom he believed in the exquisitely carved Temples, in the chanting of the pilgrims as they bathed in the holy water of the Ganges, in the flight of the birds, and even, perhaps, in the chattering of the monkeys in the blossom-covered frangipani trees.

Everywhere there was beauty. Then, from that and the love that had been so vital and inescapable in her home, she had come to England and misery.

Now at the Abbey she had found again what her father had always sought—beauty.

She would stand in front of the Marquis's painting, entranced by the loveliness of a sunset by Turner; while the rich colours of a Rubens made her think of the silks, satins, and jewels worn by the Maharajahs.

Her mind would thrill to the mystic mythology of a Poussin and the spiritual perfection of the Italian masters who had portrayed the Madonna in countless different paintings.

Kistna could remember that she had seen that same expression of sanctity on the faces of the Indian women when in their colourful *saris* they would kneel in the dust before a wayside Shrine or scatter flower-petals in the incense-filled Temples.

There was beauty too, she thought, not only in every room inside the Abbey but in the green Park with its huge ancient oak trees and in the lake, where the swans who moved over it looked like ships in full sail. Above all, there was beauty in the Marquis himself.

Never had she imagined from that first moment when she had seen him standing outside the door that any man could look more handsome, more commanding, more magnificent.

He made her think of the Governor-Generals she had seen bowling through Calcutta in a high-wheeled gilded barouche, with foot-grooms running beside it and with an escort of Cavalry behind.

She had thought then that nothing could be more dashing or more important.

But the Marquis exuded the same atmosphere of power and authority just by being himself. At the same time, omnipotent though he appeared, his kindness made her want to cry.

"How could any man be so wonderful?" she asked herself, as she touched with gentle fingers the fine lingerie trimmed with lace which Madame Yvonne had sent from London.

Never had she imagined that she would know such softness against her skin or feel as if she were wrapped in a silken web woven by fairies.

"He is wonderful! Wonderful!"

She found herself repeating the same sentence not once but a dozen times every day.

Because she wanted to please him, she strove to do everything he asked of her and to do it well, if not to exceed his requirements.

"How could I be so fortunate or so blessed as to become the Ward of such a man," she asked herself, "who lives like a King and is certainly a King among men?"

She liked Peregrine Wallingham, and she knew that if the Marquis had not been there, she would have been impressed by him.

He teased her and laughed with her and she thought him charming and good-humoured, but the Marquis was wonderful and god-like.

Looking at him riding a horse, she knew instinctively that he was a better rider and a better horseman than any other man could be.

So she tried desperately hard to ride as he would wish her to do, so that she would be a worthy companion and he would be proud of her.

There were so many things to remember and so many small points of etiquette which apparently were of importance that sometimes Kistna felt despairingly that she would fail not only the Marquis but herself.

When she made mistakes she would lie awake at night wondering how she could have been so stupid and feeling ashamed that she should have failed his demand for perfection.

Sometimes she thought of her future, but for the moment nothing seemed important except the present.

Because it had a dream-like quality, it was impossible to think ahead, except to hurry in dressing, changing, and getting through the darkness of the night so that she could see the Marquis again.

"Your hair certainly has new life in it, Miss Kistna," Mrs. Dawes said one morning.

"Are you sure?" Kistna asked.

"It's a fact, Miss," Mrs. Dawes replied.

She was brushing out Kistna's long hair, and, seeing it spring out from the brush, each hair seemed charged with a separate life of its own.

"Yes, it is better," Kistna agreed, "it really is!"

"And so are you, Miss," Mrs. Dawes answered. "I said to Ethel only yesterday: 'Miss Kistna's growing real pretty now that she has some flesh on her bones. You mark my words, she'll be a beauty before she's finished!' "

Kistna bent forward to look at herself in the mirror.

'Is that possible?' she wondered to herself; and if she was pretty, perhaps even beautiful, would the Marquis notice it?

She had been too miserable and hungry at the Orphanage to worry about how she looked. Now in the beauty of the Abbey, with the Marquis's grey eyes on her, she longed desperately to look like her mother.

There was no doubt that her mother had been beautiful and not only in the eyes of her husband, who had adored her.

As Kistna had grown older she had been aware that every Englishman who had come to their house would look at her mother, then look again, with an expression that she grew to recognise first as one of incredulity, then of admiration.

It was almost as if they said aloud:

"How, here in India, married to an obscure Missionary, could one expect to find such a beautiful woman? And one who apparently is content with what must be a very restricted life?"

Sometimes they would further a casual acquaintance by calling again and again at the small poor bungalow, arriving in luxurious carriages which belonged to the Governor with servants wearing the flamboyant red-and-white uniforms affected by the servants of the Raj.

They would start by being a little condesending, a little patronising, only to find incredibly that the beautiful Mrs. Lovell, while polite and listening attentively to what they had to say, was not the least interested in them as men.

It was then that they became more insistent and, Kistna would think, very much more sincere.

If her father came home while they were there, she often thought it should be impossible for them not to understand why her mother did not press them to stay or to come again.

When her father's footsteps sounded on the verandah, her mother would jump to her feet, and her face, beautiful though it had been before, seemed to have a new beauty which made it impossible not to watch her.

"John!"

She would breathe the word and her eyes would be shining.

Then she would run across the poorly furnished room to her husband, and even though they had been with each other only an hour or so before, his arms would go round her and he would hold her against him.

It was as if they had been reunited after a long passage of time, and Kistna, when she was old enough, began to understand that every minute they were not together did in fact seem to them a century of emptiness and frustration.

"That is love," she had said to herself, "and it is very beautiful."

It was love she missed at the Orphanage, and because there was no love, there was no beauty.

Now, at the Abbey, it was hers again, perhaps not the beauty of the love her father and mother had known, but at least the kindness and understanding of two men who apparently found her interesting and to whom in gratitude she poured out the emotions of which she had been deprived and starved for three long years.

"How do I look, Mrs. Dawes?" Kistna asked that evening.

She had put on a gown that had arrived at midday from London.

It was white, embroidered with silver thread, and Madame · Yvonne had hidden her thin arms under voluminous sleeves of diaphanous gauze speckled with silver and had draped the neck with the same gauze that shimmered in the light of the candles when she moved.

There was a velvet ribbon at the neck, on which was attached a little spray, of silver and white flowers, and there were the same flowers for her hair, from which ribbons fell down her back and were a further clever disguise for the sharpness of her bones.

"You look real pretty, Miss Kistna!" Mrs. Dawes exclaimed. "There's never been a young lady staying in this house as could hold a candle to you."

"Do you mean that?" Kistna asked. "Oh, Mrs. Dawes, I do hope you are telling me the truth."

"I can assure you, Miss Kistna, I never lie, and I'm not saying a word that could not be spoken over the Bible itself!"

"I hope His Lordship agrees with you," Kistna said almost as if she spoke to herself.

Mrs. Dawes gave her a sharp look. Then she said in a different tone:

"I'm sure His Lordship will be pleased, and soon he'll be inviting young people of your own age here to meet you, and that's as sure as sure!"

She saw Kistna look at her enquiringly, and she went on:

"I expect as soon as you are well enough His Lordship will be finding you dance-partners amongst the young gentlemen of the neighbourhood, and you'll find plenty of them in London."

"I do not want . . . dance-partners when I might dance with . . . His Lordship and Mr. Wallingham," Kistna said.

Mrs. Dawes gave a laugh that somehow sounded affected.

"Oh, it's young gentlemen I'm thinking of, like young Lord Barrowfield, who lives on the next Estate. Twenty-two he'll be next birthday, and a nicer young man it'd be hard to meet. Perhaps His Lordship will have him in mind as a husband for you."

The words startled Kistna and she turned to look at Mrs. Dawes as if she thought she could not have heard her aright.

"A . . . h-husband?"

"Yes, of course, Miss," Mrs. Dawes replied. "You're eighteen, and most young ladies want to be fixed up before their nineteenth birthday. If you're thinking there's lots of time—time soon passes."

She tidied some things on the dressing-table as she went on:

"Don't you worry your head, Miss Kistna. I'm sure His Lordship has your future in mind, and a lovely bride you'll make, really lovely! It would be nice for you to be married here at the Abbey. It's a long time since there's been a Wedding Reception in the Ball-Room."

Kistna did not answer. She merely rose to her feet and said in a voice that somehow seemed incoherent:

"I must . . . go downstairs . . . His . . . Lordship will be . . . waiting for me!"

She did not look at or speak to Mrs. Dawes again as she left the bedroom, and the Housekeeper stood watching her go, an expression on her face that was one of anxiety.

"Poor child!" she said beneath her breath. "It's what I expected would happen, and how could it be otherwise, with His Lordship so handsome and women flocking round him like flies round a honey-pot?"

Because the idea annoyed her, Mrs. Dawes set the silver-backed hair-brushes sharply down on the dressing-table.

* * *

Downstairs, Kistna paused before she entered the Salon.

She felt as if she must pull herself together, although why she should do so or what had made her feel so strange she did not wish to explain even to herself.

She only knew that she was afraid, and there were no words in which to express it.

A footman had opened the door and was looking at her wondering why she did not go into the Salon.

Then as she did so, she saw the Marquis standing at the far end in front of the mantelpiece.

Dressed in his evening-clothes, he was very impressive and, Kistna thought, very magnificent.

Then, because she would not help herself, because fear was making her heart beat in a strange way, because he was looking towards her with a smile on his lips, she felt that he stood for security and what she wanted more than anything else—beauty.

Forgetting her lessons, forgetting all he had taught her, she started to run towards him.

Chapter Five

Kistna was laughing at something Peregrine had said as the three of them rode back through the Park towards the Abbey.

It was nearly luncheon-time and Kistna had begun to feel hungry even though she disliked knowing that their ride had come to an end.

It was a joy that was inexpressible to know that every morning she could ride the Marquis's magnificent horses, and with him.

Today they had gone farther than usual and had raced each other on a flat stretch of land that was over a mile long.

It was inevitable that the Marquis should win, but Kistna managed to beat Peregrine by a short head and he congratulated her.

"Who would have thought that that miserable girl who looked like a lamp-post," he said teasingly, "and had ridden nothing better than an Indian donkey should dare to prove herself an Amazon and beat me!"

Kistna laughed.

"I am delighted I have been able to do so, and as it happens I never rode a donkey in India!"

"Then it was either an elephant or a camel," Peregrine retorted, "but certainly nothing as swift as what Linden produces from his stable."

"There I agree with you," Kistna said. "They are the most marvellous horses one could imagine, and if

I were an Amazon I would steal one and gallop away."

"Where would you go?" Peregrine asked.

Kistna had been speaking lightly, trying as she always did to out-do Peregrine in repartee.

Now, suddenly serious, she glanced at the Marquis and beneath her breath she murmured:

"Nowhere!"

Peregrine followed the direction of her eyes, and, like Mrs. Dawes, he realised at once what had happened and wondered what he should do about it.

He thought that Kistna had already suffered enough to last her a lifetime, and it would be cruel to have her break her heart as so many other women had done over the Marquis.

Peregrine better than anybody else was aware that no woman, however attractive, had ever held his attention for long.

He had the feeling, which he had never expressed before even to himself, that the Marquis was searching for some ideal, some mythical woman he would never find.

As they rode on, with Kistna edging her horse a little nearer to the Marquis's, Peregrine was wondering if he should warn her.

Then he thought it would be useless.

Love, he told himself with uncharacteristic seriousness, was something that one could not prevent or control. It happened, and when it did, there was little one could do about it.

'She is young, she will soon get over it,' he tried to think.

But he found it difficult to imagine Kistna with Branscombe.

He had not been with her every day and nearly every hour for the past ten days without realising that not only was she, as he thought at first, quick-witted, but there were also depths to her character which he had certainly not found in any other young woman of the same age.

'It is because she has lived abroad,' he thought, but he knew it was more than that, and sometimes when they were talking together he felt that Kistna was as old as, if not older than, he and the Marquis.

'It is a question of thinking and feeling,' he decided with an unusal perception.

Then at something Kistna said to him they were all laughing again and he kept them amused until the Abbey was in sight.

"What are we doing this afternoon?" Peregrine asked as they rode over the bridge that spanned the lake.

"I have planned something rather interesting," the Marquis replied, "which will be a surprise."

"I will say one thing about you, Linden," Peregrine replied, "you are a superb host. I was thinking last night, I have never had a quieter time at the Abbey or a more interesting one."

"I would not wish you to be bored," the Marquis said mockingly.

"There is no likelihood of that," Peregrine said in all sincerity.

As he spoke, he thought that it was something his host should be saying; for it was the Marquis who had been bored in London, bored at the races, bored at the last Mill they had attended, and bored with Isobel.

As they rode on towards the house they saw that there was a carriage standing outside the front door.

Peregrine looked at it casually, then as he saw its up-to-date, expensive lines and the four horses drawing it, he looked sharply at the Marquis and realised he was as aware as he was who was calling.

They reached the front door, and as the grooms came hurrying to the horses' heads, the Marquis dismounted and went to Kistna to assist her to alight.

As he did so, he said in a low voice:

"Go upstairs and stay in your room until I send for you."

Kistna's eyes widened in surprise, but he did not bother to explain and merely walked ahead up the steps and into the Hall, knowing that she would obey him.

As he handed his hat, riding-gloves, and whip to one of the footmen, the Butler said:

"Lady Isobel Sidley has called, M'Lord, and is waiting for Your Lordship in the Silver Salon."

The Marquis did not reply, and there was a scowl between his eyes as he walked in the direction of the Silver Salon, thinking that a scene was inevitable and it was impossible for him to avoid it.

Isobel was looking extremely beautiful as she rose from the chair on which she had been sitting and held out both her hands to him.

"Linden!" she said in a voice that meant she was deliberately being alluring. "I decided that as Mohammed would not come to the mountain, the mountain must come to Mohammed."

"I am surprised to see you, Isobel!" the Marquis said.

He raised one of her hands perfunctorily to his lips, then somehow extricated himself from her fingers though she was obviously trying to cling to him.

"How can you be so heartless, so cruel, as to leave London without telling me where you were going or when you would return!"

"I was not certain of that myself," the Marquis replied. "Have you really come all this way to ask me questions, or are you staying in the neighbourhood?"

"I am staying with you, or at least I hope so," Isobel replied.

She glanced at him from under her eye-lashes in a way which made most men feel the blood rush to their heads. But the Marquis appeared to be unmoved.

"I am afraid that is impossible," he said in an uncompromising voice which she knew only too well.

"Why?"

"Because Peregrine and I are here alone and I have no wish for a party.

"You are lying!"

The accusation was almost spat at the Marquis and he stiffened.

"I know you are lying," she went on. "I was told that you were out riding with Peregrine Wallingham and your Ward! I did not realise that Mirabelle Chester had arrived in England."

If the Marquis was disconcerted at Kistna's presence being revealed, he did not show it. Instead he said:

"Mirabelle is still a School-girl and cannot even be considered a débutante until she has made her curtsey to the Queen at Buckingham Palace."

"People have been talking of her arrival in this country and of her great foutune."

"People will talk about anything," the Marquis remarked in a lofty tone. "But I must persuade you to return to London this afternoon, even though it may seem inhospitable."

"I want to be with you," Isobel insisted, and now she was pouting.

"Then I am delighted to invite you to stay to luncheon, but as I have just returned from riding, I must go and change."

Lady Isobel moved a little nearer to him.

"Let me stay the night, Linden," she begged in a low voice. "I want to talk to you, and be with you."

The invitation in her dark eyes was very obvious but the Marquis was already walking towards the door.

"I am sure Peregrine will be delighted to entertain you with a glass of champagne," he said, "and you must tell him all the gossip that has accumulated since we have been away from London."

He walked out of the Salon and saw Peregrine halfway up the stairs.

He waited, and as the Marquis caught up with him he said:

"What does she want? Or is that an unnecessary question?"

"I have told her she can stay to luncheon but must leave this afternoon," the Marquis replied. "She has been told that Mirabelle is here, and I am going to tell Kistna to have luncheon upstairs. I have told Isobel she is only a school-girl and not yet entitled to be treated as a débutante."

Peregrine raised his eye-brows but said nothing, and the Marquis went on:

"I am going now to tell her to keep out of sight, and then I must change my clothes. But there is no need for you to change yours, so go and ply Isobel with champagne! If she asks you about Mirabelle, say indifferently that she is nothing but a School-girl who will need a lot of grooming before she appears in Society."

The Marquis did not wait for an answer but hurried up the stairs two at a time.

Peregrine, with a twinkle in his eyes, turned and went down again.

'I might have anticipated,' he thought, 'that this sort of situation would arise.'

It amused him to see how the Marquis was striving to keep control of events, though he might soon find that beyond his power.

The Marquis went to Kistna's bedroom and knocked on the door.

She said: "Come in!" but when he entered she did not turn her head.

She was standing looking out the window, and although she had taken off her hat, she obviously had not rung for her maid or begun to change her riding-habit for a gown.

She was in fact wondering who Lady Isobel was, being certain in her own mind that she was someone who loved the Marquis and whom perhaps he loved in return.

"Kistna!"

As the Marquis spoke her name Kistna started and turned round.

She had been expecting a maid, and when she saw him standing just inside the door there was a sudden light in her eyes and a radiance in her face which made it seem as if the sunshine had come inside the room.

For a moment the Marquis looked at her. Then, as if he remembered why he was there, he said:

"Somebody has called to see me whom I am

anxious you should not meet. I therefore wish you to
have luncheon up here in your *Boudoir*. As soon as
she has gone I will send a message to let you know
and you can come downstairs."

Having given his instructions, he would have
turned away, but Kistna asked:

"Why should I not ... meet this ... lady? Are you
... ashamed of me?"

"No, of course not!" the Marquis answered quickly. "It is nothing like that."

"Then ... why am I to stay ... out of sight?"

"One reason," he explained, "is that you are staying in the Abbey unchaperoned. You must be aware
that it would be correct for an elderly or married
woman to be present."

Because she had expected a different answer, the
radiance which had faded from Kistna's face when
the Marquis had first told her what she was to do was
back again.

"Is that all?" she asked in such a tone of relief
that he looked at her curiously.

"What else did you expect?"

What Kistna had really thought was that the
Marquis wanted to be alone with the lady who had
called. It was an inexpressible relief to know that his
reason was merely a conventional one, and she said:

"Of course I will have my luncheon up here as
you want me to, but please, My Lord, do not let your
visitor ... spoil the afternoon. I am so looking forward
to the ... surprise you have planned."

She was suddenly very child-like in the way she
pleaded with him, and the Marquis smiled as he
answered:

"I promise you I will do my best."

Yet, as he left her he had the feeling that he was
being unkind, and when he went downstairs again he
was very conscious of the fact that there was a lonely
young woman eating alone while Isobel was waiting
for him.

Luncheon was in fact an uncomfortable meal,
because Lady Isobel was determined to hold the

attention of the Marquis and undoubtedly resented Peregrine being there.

She made spiteful replies to some of the things he said, and when he lapsed into silence and the Marquis made no effort to talk, Isobel attempted to keep the conversation concentrated on herself but was not very successful at it.

Instead of the lavish meal usually served at the Abbey, Peregrine suspected that the Marquis had cancelled at least two courses, because luncheon was finished far quicker than was usual.

"I will order your carriage, Isobel," he said as he rose from the table.

"I wish to speak to you alone, Linden."

She walked with an air of defiance towards the Silver Salon.

As she entered it the Marquis hung back for a moment to say to Peregrine:

"Order her carriage. I only hope this will not take long."

"I am sorry for you," Peregrine replied.

The Marquis closed the Salon door behind him and moved towards his guest in a casual manner.

At the same time, he was uncomfortably aware that Isobel was determined to have a scene.

However, she tried a different tactic from what he had expected by throwing herself precipitately into his arms the moment he reached her side.

"Oh, Linden, I love you!" she said, lifting her lips to his. "Kiss me, and I will tell you how much."

The Marquis looked down at her beautiful face and as he did so he realised that she no longer had the slightest attraction for him.

In fact, it was difficult to remember why he had ever found her irresistibly fascinating or how in the past she had easily managed to evoke a fiery response from him by an overture such as this.

With an ease which came from long experience of evading clinging women, the Marquis managed to extricate himself from Lady Isobel's arms.

"I think, Isobel," he said, as he stood with his back to the fireplace, "we are both old enough and experienced enough to know when an *affaire de coeur* such as we have both enjoyed comes to an end."

"There is no question of it coming to an end as far as I am concerned."

Lady Isobel's voice rose a little as she spoke, and the Marquis was aware that she was angry because he had avoided her wiles.

"What I suggest," he said, "is that when I return to London I will give you a present that will commemorate the very happy times we have spent together in the past. And I hope there will be no recriminations or regrets and that we shall always be friends."

As he spoke, he thought that what he had said sounded priggish and slightly pompous, but he knew from past experience that there was really nothing else he could say to a woman who still wanted him while he had no further interest in her.

But while many of his discarded loves had wept, sulked, or merely accepted the inevitable, Isobel was made of sterner stuff.

Having been spoilt all her life and having a very inflated idea of her own charms, she was not only furious at losing the Marquis but was also insulted that he no longer desired her as a woman.

Incensed almost beyond control, she spat out her venom at him, berating him in a manner that he thought would not have come amiss in a Billingsgate fish-wife, and with every second that passed he found her more unpleasant.

By the time she finished he had come to the conclusion that he positively disliked her and had decided that there was no-one to blame but himself for having had the bad taste to find her desirable in the first place.

When finally Isobel could find nothing more to say and had already repeated herself a dozen times, she picked up her gloves and her reticule and said in a bitter and acid voice:

"I will leave you, Linden, as you are so anxious for me to do so, but let me make this absolutely clear—I loathe and detest you for what you have done to me! I gave you my heart and you trampled it under your feet. One day you will be paid back in your own coin."

Her eyes narrowed as she went on:

"One day you will suffer and some woman will hurt you as I have been hurt, and I shall rejoice that she has the power to do so!"

The Marquis did not reply. He merely inclined his head.

Then with a violent sound of exasperation Lady Isobel swept down the Salon towards the door. The Marquis followed her slowly, thinking only how glad he would be to see the last of her.

They reached the Hall where one of the footmen was waiting with the silk pelisse that matched the gown Lady Isobel was wearing.

As she allowed the flunkey to help her into it, she looked up at the ceiling in the Hall, then down to where the flags hung over the mantelpiece and to the Marquis standing waiting for her to leave.

She was, in her heart, cursing the Abbey and the owner of it, but to Kistna peeping at her through the bannisters she looked so exquisitely beautiful that it was an indescribable agony to see her.

Never had Kistna thought that any woman could look so lovely or be so exquisitely gowned.

Her bonnet trimmed with ostrich-feathers and her gown with huge sleeves and a full skirt gave Lady Isobel a glamour and an elegance which had made her the undisputed toast of St. James's.

'She is the most beautiful person I have ever seen, and the exact . . . counterpart to the . . . Marquis,' Kistna thought.

Then as if she could not bear to go on looking at the woman below, she ran back along the passage to her own Sitting-Room, wishing that her curiosity had not made her leave it.

It had, however, been impossible for her to resist her desire to see the reason why she must have luncheon alone.

Now she could understand why the Marquis would not want a complete stranger to be present when he talked intimately to somebody belonging to his world, as she would never be able to do.

"I am just an ... outsider," Kistna whispered to herself.

She felt she could see nothing but Lady Isobel's beautiful face, and the picture she made with her eyes looking upwards at the ceiling, then descending slowly to rest on the Marquis, was, Kistna thought, engraved on her heart.

She felt a pain that seemed to strike into her like a dagger.

Then as she felt as if even the beauty of the Abbey could no longer help her, nor the sunshine outside, nor the pretty gown she was wearing, the ugliness was back in her life, and this time it lay within herself.

It was the ugliness of pain, and she recognised it for what it was: the pain of jealousy.

"How can I be jealous of a woman I have seen only for a fleeting second?" she asked herself.

But she knew the answer.

She was jealous because she loved the Marquis and he filled her whole life!

She supposed she should have known the truth a long time ago and acknowledged it. Now she felt almost as if it struck her like a blow.

And yet it was so inevitable, already so much a part of her living and breathing, that it was almost absurd to think she had not been aware of it.

Of course she loved him! She had loved him from the very first moment when she had seen him standing outside the front door of the Orphanage.

She had loved him even while she had been blaming him for the agony they had suffered from Mrs. Moore.

She had loved him when he had put things right, and when he had fetched her that first morning to take her to the Abbey.

She had lain awake the first night fearing that the promise he had made was something he would never substantiate.

"He did not mean it," her rational mind had tried to tell her.

But her heart believed him, because already she loved him. He was St. Michael coming to save her, attended by his angels, and she was ready to go down on her knees and worship him.

She knew now that her love had grown more and more every day and every minute that she had been with the Marquis.

She had awakened each day with a feeling of wild excitement because as soon as she was dressed and downstairs she would see him.

She had gone to sleep thinking of him, to dream of him, and when she awoke she thought of him again.

"I love him! I love him!" she said now, a hundred times, as she walked restlessly round the attractive flower-filled *Boudoir* which opened out of her bedroom.

When she had first seen it she had thought it was the loveliest room one could ever imagine. Now it seemed like a cage, a prison which kept her from being with the Marquis when he was somewhere else.

She had a sudden fear that if the beautiful lady was going back to London, the Marquis would go with her. Then even as the thought seemed to shoot through her, leaving a streak of pain behind, there was a knock on the door.

With difficulty Kistna managed to answer.

"His Lordship's compliments, Miss," one of the footmen said, "and he wishes you to join him ready to go driving."

Kistna felt her heart leap.

She ran into the bedroom to put on a pretty bonnet that went with the gown she was wearing and to pick up a silk shawl and her gloves which the maid had left ready on one of the chairs.

Only as she ran towards the door did a sudden thought take her instead to the dressing-table to look at herself in the mirror.

For a moment she did not see her own reflection

but the beautiful face she had seen below in the Hall, and with difficulty she prevented herself from giving a cry of despair.

How could she be so silly? How could she expect for one moment that the Marquis would so much as notice her when there were lovely women who looked like angels competing for his favours?

"It is hopeless!" Kistna told herself despairingly.

At the same time, she was feminine enough to realise that now that her eyes were no longer sunken in her head they looked very large, almost too large for her face, and as her cheeks had filled out her mouth seemed smaller and properly curved.

Her chin was still a sharp line but her neck was round, and her skin was smooth and no longer sallow but white.

She stared at herself for a few seconds, then turned away because she had only one thought in her mind—to be with the Marquis!

She seemed to fly rather than walk down the stairs to where he would be waiting for her.

* * *

"You realise," Peregrine said later that evening when Kistna had gone to bed, "that Isobel will undoubtedly tell all London that Mirabelle has arrived. That means that Branscombe will be on our tracks."

"I have thought of that," the Marquis replied. "The best thing we can do is to sit tight and let Branscombe make the first move."

"You are quite certain he will do so?"

"I do not believe he would change his intention so quickly, unless he has come into a fortune in the meantime."

"I cannot understand how he can possibly need money," Peregrine said, "but if he does, then Mirabelle Chester is obviously the answer to his dreams."

As he spoke, Peregrine noticed that there was almost a cruel smile on the Marquis's lips, and he knew without being told that his friend was thinking of the satisfaction he would feel if their plot succeeded and they made the Earl look a fool.

"We have little more than a week before Ascot," he remarked, "and if Branscombe has not come up to scratch by then, what do you intend to do about Kistna?"

"I am quite certain he will not let the grass grow under his feet," the Marquis replied. "In fact, with Isobel abusing me from the roof-tops you may be quite certain that we shall have some response from him within the next twenty-four hours."

"You are very optimistic."

"I do not make many mistakes when dealing with men of Branscombe's calibre," the Marquis said. "And I consider myself to be a good judge of character."

He spoke with a tone of satisfaction, then as he met Peregrine's eyes he laughed a little ruefully.

"That only applies to one sex," he said. "I admit where Isobel is concerned I made a grave error of judgement."

"No-one, unless he is a magician, can ever be sure what a woman will be like," Peregrine said consolingly, "and if they all ran according to form, they would certainly be boring! It is their unpredictability that makes the chase a gamble from start to finish!"

"I agree with you," the Marquis said with a smile. "At the same time, I can promise you I shall be very much more careful in the future!"

"I doubt it," Peregrine said. "But thank goodness you are at least human when it comes to women!"

"What do you mean by that?"

"I mean," Peregrine replied, "that you are too damned successful in every other way, and it is a sheer relief to ordinary mortals like myself to find that one of his gods has feet of clay!"

"Hardly a very apt metaphor," the Marquis remarked. "At the same time, it expresses the truth and I must accept it. I only hope I am not so easily taken in another time."

There was silence, then Peregrine said:

"What really conerns me at the moment is what you are going to do about Kistna."

"Kistna?" the Marquis queried. "You know exactly what I am going to do about her. Marry her off to

Branscombe, and watch him discover what it is like to be tricked and cheated!"

There was silence. Then Peregrine said:

"I presume you realise that if he is angry he will take it out on her?"

"I have thought of that already," the Marquis replied, "and I shall make sure he provides for her."

"In what way?"

"I am going to make him settle money on her before I give my permission for the marriage."

"Will he not think that rather strange, when the alleged Mirabelle is a thousand times richer than he is?"

"I will make my request sound convincing," the Marquis said, and his voice was hard.

Again there was a pause before Peregrine said:

"I suppose if Kistna gets some money and an undoubtedly distinguished title she will think the bargain worthwhile."

"Good God, Peregrine, why should she be anything but delighted?" the Marquis asked. "You saw the condition she was in when we found her and how much she enjoys having pretty gowns. Well, I will see that she can afford them for the rest of her life, and there is certainly no reason for her to go hungry in the future."

Peregrine felt he could say no more.

The question in his mind was whether Kistna would find that enough.

He was quite certain that she was already in love with the Marquis. The signs were all too obviously there, but once again he told himself that as she was very young, she would forget.

Besides, the Earl was a very presentable, good-looking man.

Glancing at the Marquis sitting opposite him on the other side of the hearth-rug, he wondered if he was really as obtuse as he appeared, and if it had never struck him that the girl was in love with him.

Then he told himself that the Marquis was too busy concentrating on having his revenge on the Earl to be concerned with anything else.

At the same time, Peregrine did not like to think of Kistna being unhappy.

He had learnt these last days how sensitive she was to everything the Marquis said or even thought, and he knew that after what she had been through in the Orphanage she would find it hard, if not impossible, to live in a house however grand where she was hated and despised.

'What will she feel when she knows she has been part of a plot and that Linden's generosity was merely a means to an end?' Peregrine wondered to himself.

Yet somehow it was impossible to say so to the Marquis, or to let him think that he was beginning to disapprove of his whole plan of revenge.

"We had better go to bed," the Marquis said unexpectedly. "We have to be ready for tomorrow, when anything might happen. I intend first thing to warn the household that they are not to mention Kistna as they did today when Isobel arrived, and that if anyone asks for Miss Mirabelle Chester, they are referring to her."

"When are you going to tell Kistna of the part she has to play?" Peregrine enquired.

"I was going to tell her tonight," the Marquis answered, "but it seemed to me she was a little under the weather. She appeared rather quieter than usual and not as happy as she had been all day."

Peregrine had also noticed that, but he was surprised the Marquis had.

"What do you think has upset her?" he asked.

"Why should she be upset?" the Marquis parried.

"I thought perhaps she might have resented having been sent upstairs when Isobel arrived."

"I explained that it was because she was here unchaperoned, and she seemed to think it was quite a reasonable excuse."

"It is a good thing Isobel did not see her," Peregrine said. "She would have been quite convinced that you had taken on a new love before being free of the old."

The Marquis laughed.

"A ridiculous idea, but one which would undoubtedly occur to Isobel. She would never believe I was interested in any woman unless I found her desirable."

Peregrine was silent for a moment, then he said:

"I am rather sorry in a way that we are not taking our *protégée* to London and letting her have a run for her money before she gets tied up with Branscombe."

"Why should you want to do that?" the Marquis asked.

"Because it would be interesting to see if she was as successful as I am sure she would be."

He saw that the Marquis did not understand, and he exclaimed:

"Good God, Linden, you must realise by now how attractive she is! Her eyes are fantastic, and now that her face has filled out, the rest of her features have fallen into place. Personally, I find her straight little nose entrancing! It certainly looks as blue-blooded as anything the Chesters can produce."

He spoke lightly, but there was no doubt that the Marquis was scowling at him.

"Now listen, Peregrine," he said. "If I find you messing about with Kistna I will murder you! We have taken all this trouble over her for one reason and one reason only!"

"I was only intimating that there are quite a number of men who would not only find her attractive but would be willing to marry her. So if Branscombe fails to come up to scratch, we can always let her find a man she can love."

The Marquis rose to his feet.

"I do not know what has got into you, Peregrine," he said. "You have been helpful and understanding up to now. I cannot think why you are putting obstacles in my way at the last minute."

"I am doing nothing of the sort!" Peregrine protested. "I am only saying that knowing what we do about Branscombe, we also know that anyone as sweet-natured and sensitive as Kistna is too good for him, and I wish it were possible to marry her to somebody we both like and admire."

"Get it into your head," the Marquis said sharply, "that Branscombe may cheat on race-courses and behave like an outsider in many ways, but he is still of great distinction and a favourite of the King. Can you imagine any woman not being delighted and extremely grateful at finding herself married to such a man?"

"I hope you are right," Peregrine replied. "I just feel that Kistna is different."

"It is useless to discuss this any further," the Marquis retorted, "and I forbid you, I absolutely forbid you to upset Kistna in any way. Do you understand?"

The Marquis did not wait for Peregrine's answer but walked out of the Library.

Peregrine gave a sigh.

He had never known the Marquis to be so unpredictable or indeed so bad-tempered when they were talking intimately.

He rose from his chair and stretched himself.

'I expect Linden is right,' he thought, 'and he is providing for the girl in an extremely generous manner.'

Nevertheless, as he went up to bed and there was no sign of the Marquis to say good-night to him, he had the feeling that a volcano might erupt at any moment.

* * *

In her own room, Kistna was awake, lying in the darkness, finding it impossible to sleep.

Normally she was so happy with her thoughts of the Marquis and the things they had done during the day that she would fall asleep immediately.

But tonight she could think only of her love for him and of the beautiful lady who had visited him for luncheon and whom she had not been allowed to meet.

She told herself she had been stupid to think even for a moment that the wonder and delight of being alone with the Marquis could continue.

She did not question at first how strange it was that he should stay in the country with only Peregrine

and herself, rather than be with his friends and the
King at this particular time of year when London was
gayer than at any other time.

Because she had been curious, she had talked to
Peregrine about the things they did when they were
in London, and he had told her about the Marquis's
house filled with treasures, of his importance in the
Social World, and of his skill and success at every
sport.

She had of course been intensely interested in his
successes on the Turf, but although Peregrine had
told her his horse had dead-heated for first place in
the Derby Stakes, he had not added that it was due to
the crooked riding of the Earl's jockey.

He had been aware as he talked that Kistna
listened to him with wide, excited eyes because he
was speaking of the Marquis.

"Why has His Lordship never ... married?" she
asked.

Peregrine shrugged his shoulders.

"It is not for want of trying on the part of almost
every unattached woman he meets, but he does not
fall in love with them, not to the extent of wanting to
be tied."

There was a silence, then Kistna said:

"Would he be very ... bored?"

Peregrine laughed.

"He would! And the truth is that the Marquis,
like myself, enjoys being a bachelor. We have a great
deal of fun together, and quite frankly it is more
amusing to entertain a pretty woman one night and
change her for an even prettier one the next, than to
be tied to somebody who, pretty or ugly, is a wife for
life."

Peregrine was talking in the amusing manner
which always made those who listened to him laugh.

Then he realised that Kistna was taking him very
seriously.

"I suppose I understand that," she said, "but if
one were in love ... really in love ... one would want
to be with the same person all the time ... and not
keep changing."

She was thinking of her father and mother as she spoke, and without thinking Peregrine answered:

"The Marquis likes a change—and who shall blame him? If you could fill a huge stable with the finest horses, why should you ride the same one every day and neglect the others?"

Again he was speaking lightly and frivolously. Then as he saw the expression on Kistna's face and remembered she was a Parson's daughter, he added:

"Perhaps one day the Marquis will find the right woman and so shall I. Then we shall settle down and be extremely dull and doubtless very pompous."

"There is no reason why you should be that."

Again Peregrine did not realise that Kistna was thinking of her father and mother and how when they were together they always found everything delightful and enjoyable because they could share it.

Peregrine thought he had somehow been indiscreet, and, trying to smooth things over, he said:

"There is no reason to worry your head about me or the Marquis. All you have to do is to concentrate on yourself, and when we find you a nice husband, you will undoubtedly find marriage a very enjoyable institution."

"But you have just said that most men do not wish to be married," Kistna replied, "and perhaps no-one will . . . want to marry me."

"I can assure you they will," Peregrine answered, "and if you had any money and I could afford it, I would bet you that by this time next year you would be a respectable married lady with a gold ring on your finger!"

Kistna laughed and shook her head.

"Who would want to marry me?" she asked.

Then as if she suddenly remembered something, she added:

"Except, of course . . . if I am the Ward of . . . somebody very important . . . I suppose that would count as a very . . . considerable advantage."

"It certainly will," Peregrine agreed.

Because he felt he was getting involved in a conversation he should never have started in the first place, he had been relieved when the Marquis appeared.

Kistna had gone over the conversation in her mind that night, and the nights that followed.

Now she thought that as the Marquis did not wish to get married, she would perhaps be able to stay with him for a long time and they could be happy as they were now.

Because it was something she wanted more than she had ever wanted anything, she found herself praying:

"Please, God, let me stay here with him. Please make him content to be in the country and not want to follow that beautiful lady to London."

Then as she thought of her father and mother and how deeply they had loved each other and how the very air round them had seemed somehow redolent with love when they were together, she knew that was how she loved the Marquis.

"I love him with my mind . . . my heart, and my . . . soul," she whispered into the darkness.

Then, although it seemed wicked and presumptive, she added:

"Please, God . . . let him care for me a little . . . just a very . . . little . . . and even if his love only lasts a week . . . a month . . . a year, then I could . . . die having known . . . real happiness."

Chapter Six

When they came back from riding, the Marquis said to Kistna:

"When you have changed I want to speak to you. I will be in the Library."

Because there was a note in his voice that did not sound normal, she looked at him in surprise.

Then when he did not wait for her reply but walked away in the direction of the Library, she ran upstairs.

While she was changing into what she thought was one of the prettiest gowns Madame Yvonne had sent her, Kistna wondered what the Marquis had to say to her.

She could not imagine she had done anything wrong, but she thought now that this morning when they were riding he had been a little aloof and more silent than he had been on other rides.

Peregrine had made her laugh but the Marquis had not joined, and now she was afraid that something was wrong.

"What could I have done? What could I have said?" she asked herself.

She could find no obvious answer, and as she went downstairs there was a look of anxiety in her eyes.

As Peregrine had said to the Marquis, her eyes were now not only very expressive but also beautiful, and they seemed to dominate her whole face so that it was difficult to notice her other features, good though they were.

She opened the door of the Library and went in to find the Marquis, as she had expected, sitting at the huge flat-topped desk in the centre of the room.

There was a gold ink-pot on it, made in the time of Charles II by one of the greatest goldsmiths in the land, and Kistna admired it every time she saw it.

Now she could see only the Marquis, and as always she felt her heart give a sudden leap at the sight of him, then seem to beat more quickly within her breast.

She walked towards him, but he did not look up until she stood directly in front of him.

Then he said:

"Sit down, Kistna. I have something to say to you."

Because she was nervous, she sat on the very edge of the chair and clasped her hands together.

It seemed to her that the Marquis looked at her searchingly for a long moment before he said:

"I have decided your future, which would be a very brilliant one for any young woman, but I need your help in assuring it."

He paused, and because Kistna felt he was waiting for her to reply, she said in a voice he could barely hear:

"W-what do you . . . want me to . . . do?"

"I expect like all women you have been wondering, now that you are eighteen, whom you will marry. Of course, in the circumstances in which I found you, it was unlikely you would ever meet a man, let alone one suitable to be your husband."

"I . . . I have no . . . wish to be . . . m-married," Kistna said quickly.

She saw the frown between the Marquis's eyes before he said sharply:

"That is an absurd statement for anyone of your intelligence. Of course you wish to be married, and as your Guardian I have in fact chosen a suitable husband for you."

Kistna gave an audible gasp. Then she went very pale and clenched her fingers together.

As if he knew it was impossible for her to speak, the Marquis continued:

"Because you are my Ward, and because I feel I must recompense you for your sufferings in the Orphanage, I have chosen as your husband a man who will give you what is undoubtedly the most brilliant social position in England today."

Again he paused, and he realised as he looked across the desk that Kistna was staring at him with huge frightened eyes that seemed to fill her whole face.

It struck him that there was a stricken expression in them. Then he told himself that he was being absurd and her expression was merely one of astonishment.

"The man I am talking about," the Marquis continued, "is the Earl of Branscombe. He is the possessor of an ancient and noble title, he is a sportsman of high repute on the Turf, and he enjoys the trust and friendship of the King and Queen."

The Marquis waited, and this time it was obvious that he expected Kistna to make some response.

After some seconds had passed she asked incoherently:

"W-why should he ... wish to ... marry me?"

"Because he thinks you are my Ward," the Marquis replied, and his voice was hard, "and while I do not consider the Ward he had in mind suitable for him, I feel that you, as another Ward of mine, will make him an admirable wife."

"But ... but he might not ... like me ... and I might not like ... him," Kistna stammered.

"You must be aware," the Marquis said loftily, "that in the aristocratic families in England, as in the East where you have lived, marriages are always arranged."

"But in India," Kistna said, "and ... I suspect in England, the marriages are arranged because both the bridegroom and the bride obtain some ... financial advantage from the ... union."

For a moment the Marquis was taken aback.

Then he thought he might have guessed that Kistna was too intelligent not to be aware that an arranged marriage was a business transaction from which both sides benefitted.

It took him a second or two to find the answer, but finally he said:

"The Earl of Branscombe considers that because you are my Ward, that is the advantage he requires."

"How can he want to marry somebody he has never seen ... and whom he does not ... love?"

"I have already explained to you that this is an arranged marriage," the Marquis said with a note of irritation in his voice, "and as the Earl is a very prepossessing man, and you are a very attractive young woman, love will come with marriage, if that is what you want."

He spoke as if it was something completely unimportant, but Kistna, thinking of her father and mother, said in a frightened voice:

"Please ... I do not ... wish to ... marry in such ... circumstances."

The Marquis leant back in his chair.

"That remark is foolish and over-emotional," he said. "You must be aware that I am offering you a marriage which would be the height of the ambitions of any girl in England, and to most of them it would be an alliance beyond their wildest dreams."

He looked at Kistna almost angrily as he continued:

"Surely you have not forgotten already the condition you were in when I found you at the Orphanage? You said at the time it might only have been a question of a year or even a few months before you died from starvation and cold. In contrast, what could be more advantageous from every point of view than for you to become the Countess of Branscombe?"

Because Kistna could not bear to see the anger in his eyes she looked away from him and stared down at her hands. She felt as if the irritation in his voice vibrated through her body, making her feel almost as if he hurt her physically.

"Apart from anything else," the Marquis went on, "I think you should be grateful to me for giving you the opportunity of such a golden future."

"I am ... very grateful ... for everything you have ... done for me," Kistna said, and now there was a sob in her voice.

"Then if you are grateful," the Marquis answered, "you will do what I tell you to do, without making difficulties. I cannot think that is too much to ask."

There was a pause. Then Kistna said:

"I am ... grateful, My Lord ... and I will do what you ... tell me to do."

"Good!" the Marquis approved. "Now listen carefully."

He bent forward with his arms on the desk as if to intensify the importance of what he was about to say.

"The Earl of Branscombe has already announced in London that he intends to marry my Ward. When he arrives here I shall introduce you to him as my Ward, which indeed you are. But he has no idea that you even exist and he has asked in fact for my other Ward, who is in Italy at the moment. Her name is Mirabelle Chester, and that is who you will let him think you are."

Kistna raised her head.

"Do you mean ... I am to ... deceive him?" she enquired.

"What does it matter?" the Marquis asked lightly. "One Ward is as good as another."

"I do not ... understand! Why should we not tell him my ... real name?"

"Because," the Marquis said slowly, "I wish him to believe that you are Mirabelle Chester, and I am asking you to help me and yourself by doing what I require."

There was silence. Then Kistna said:

"But ... will you not explain to me ... why this ... deception is necessary?"

"No," the Marquis said firmly. "It is my business and mine alone. As I have already pointed out, Kistna, I am ensuring that your future will be one which

ranks high in the Social World and you will be the
envy of every other young woman. What more can
you want?"

To the Marquis's surprise, Kistna rose from her
chair and walked away towards the window.

He found himself, without meaning to, admiring
the grace of the way she moved and the lines of her
figure. She wore a gown of pale pink gauze trimmed
with ribbons of the same colour.

'She is like a flower,' he thought, then told himself
sharply that she was being difficult.

With her back to him, Kistna stood looking out at
the sunshine on the Park. Then she said:

"Will you be very ... angry if I ... refuse to do
what you ... want?"

The Marquis started, then brought his hand
down sharply on the desk in front of him.

"I will not only be angry," he replied, "but I
should think you half-witted, which is something I
have never thought before."

Kistna did not speak or look round and he went
on:

"If you will not marry Branscombe as I wish you
to do, have you thought of the alternative? You can
hardly stay here with me indefinitely, unchaperoned
and with nothing to look forward to except an attempt
to find another husband. It would certainly be impossible for me to produce one who could equal the Earl
in any way."

"I could perhaps ... earn my own ... living."

"How?" the Marquis enquired. "What talents
have you for earning money in a very competitive
world?"

She did not reply and he went on:

"Perhaps you are thinking of working in an Orphanage, but I should have thought you would have
had enough of that sort of existence, even in one
better equipped than the place where I found you."

Again Kistna felt almost as if he had hit her, and
because she knew she could not bear him to be angry
with her, she turned back to say:

"I am ... grateful for your kindness and for ...

thinking of me ... and I will try to ... do what you ... want."

Her voice broke a little on the last word, but she controlled herself and as she stood in front of him at the desk, the Marquis said:

"I thought you would see sense. Now, remember, Kistna, that your name is Mirabelle Chester. You are the daughter of my cousin Lionel, who was a wanderer over the face of the earth—I think he called himself an explorer—but he is dead and his wife is dead also."

"So Mirabelle is an ... orphan ... like me!"

"Exactly!" the Marquis said. "In fact, as you are the same age you will see that you have several things in common."

He looked at Kistna as he spoke and thought she looked very pale, almost as if she might faint.

He rose to his feet.

"Come and sit down in a comfortable chair," he suggested, "and I will tell you more about Mirabelle so that you do not make any mistakes."

He walked from behind the desk towards the fireplace and Kistna followed him slowly to sit down on one of the big comfortable armchairs.

Because it had been so warm for the last two days, the fire was not lit. Instead, the fireplace was filled with a magnificent arrangement of flowers and plants from the Marquis's own greenhouses.

Kistna could smell their fragrance and she thought it was very much part of the beauty of the Abbey and very different from the smell of the dust, dirt, and misery she had known at the Orphanage.

Living in India had taught her to use her senses and she thought that it was not only what one could see and hear which made a picture in the mind that remained in the memory, but also the smell of places and even people.

To her the Abbey had a scent that was a mixture of the fragrances of flowers, bees'-wax, cigar-smoke, and the cleanness of the fresh air outside.

It was all associated in her mind with the Marquis, and as he sat down opposite her, he looked so handsome and so irresistibly attractive that she felt her whole body vibrate with love.

"Mirabelle, since her father died, has been living in Rome," he was saying, "and finishing her studies at a very good School. But I expect you will find that you know quite as much as she does and perhaps, because you have experienced a very different life, in many ways you know even more."

"I do not ... speak Italian."

"No, but your French is coming along," the Marquis replied, "and I think it is very unlikely that the Earl speaks any foreign language except French."

"Suppose he ... asks me questions I cannot ... answer?"

"I imagine you are quick-witted enough to avoid being caught out," the Marquis said, "and it is always best in such circumstances to say as little as possible."

"When are you ... planning I should ... be married?" Kistna asked.

The Marquis was just about to reply: "As soon as possible!" when he thought that might frighten her.

Instead he answered deliberately vaguely:

"We shall have to discuss that, of course, with the Earl, and I suggest you leave the arrangements in my hands. Just think how very lucky you are, and that if your father and mother were alive they too would be grateful to me for taking care of your future in an exceptional manner of which they could not help approving."

The Marquis thought as he spoke that he was being somewhat ponderous but undoubtedly reassuring.

What he did not expect was that Kistna should look at him wildly, as though she was going to protest or say something that might cancel out everything she had agreed to before.

Then, as if with a tremendous effort, her expression changed, but the tears came into her eyes and made them look even bigger than they were already.

With an incoherent little word of apology, she rose from the chair and ran from the room, leaving the Marquis staring after her until he could no longer hear her footsteps running down the passage.

* * *

"A visitor!" Peregrine exclaimed as they drove down the drive.

He looked at the Marquis as he spoke and they simultaneously knew whose Phaeton was standing outside the door of the Abbey.

When they drew a little nearer there was no mistaking the yellow-and-black wheels and upholstery, while the same colours were echoed in the coachman's livery, which were also the Earl's racing colours.

"Who do you think it can be?" Kistna asked. "And do you want me to . . . hide until they . . . leave?"

There was a little tremor in her voice as she asked the question, because she thought that perhaps the beautiful lady who had called on the Marquis yesterday morning had returned.

They had driven over to one of the farms in the Marquis's Phaeton and Kistna had been entranced by the newly born lambs and the calves that were just able to stand on their spindly legs.

Because she had been so happy to be with the Marquis, she had for the moment forgotten her unhappiness of the morning, and she had found everything at the farm so entrancing that her enthusiasm had communicated itself both to the Marquis and to Peregrine.

"Mama told me how beautiful spring was in England," she said. "But although I expected golden daffodils under the trees, and the shrubs and hedges coming into bud, I had forgotten there would be lambs like this and fluffy yellow chicks and waddling baby ducks!"

She picked up a little yellow chick as she spoke and held it in the palm of her hand for the Marquis to look at it.

"Could anything be more adorable?" she asked.

Watching her, Peregrine thought the same adjective might apply to her, and he wondered why the Marquis did not realise how attractive she looked with the chick in her hand and her eyes soft yet radiant with happiness.

Now the happiness was dimmed as Kistna looked ahead.

"What I want you to do," the Marquis said, and there was a definite note of satisfaction in his voice, "is to go upstairs and put on your prettiest and most expensive-looking gown. Get your maid to arrange your hair, and be ready when I send for you to meet your future husband, the Earl of Branscombe."

"He is . . . here?"

There was no doubt of the dismay in Kistna's voice.

"That is his Phaeton," the Marquis replied. "As you see, it is a very expensive vehicle, and I direct your attention to his horses, which are always outstanding!"

There was a little sting in the way he spoke, and Kistna looked at him.

She did not speak, and after a moment he said:

"You promised to do what I ask you, Kistna! Be careful to remember that your name is Mirabelle, which is how I shall address you."

"I have . . . not forgotten," Kistna said in a low voice, "but I was wondering why . . . when you wish me to marry him . . . you do not . . . like the Earl."

"Who said I did not like him?"

"I heard it . . . in your voice."

"I think you are being over-imaginative," the Marquis said coldly.

They had reached the gravel sweep outside the front door and he drew his horses to a standstill behind the Phaeton belonging to the Earl.

They stepped out, and because she knew she must obey orders Kistna hurried up the staircase to her room.

The Marquis turned to Peregrine with a smile on his lips.

"You were right!" he said in a voice the servants could not hear. "The fish has risen to the fly and now all we have to do is to land him!"

"I will leave you to do that," Peregrine replied, "but just remember one thing, Linden."

"What is that?"

"You are playing a game with people, not chess-men."

The Marquis looked at him in perplexity but Peregrine had already turned away and was climbing the stairs towards his own room.

A footman opened the door of the Salon where the Earl was waiting.

As the Marquis entered he saw him at the far end and was instantly aware of a feeling of dislike and distrust.

But he appeared both genial and surprised as he moved forward to say:

"Good-afternoon, Branscombe! This is an unexpected visit!"

"I was on my way to stay with Verulam at Gorhambury," the Earl replied. "As I wished to see you on a personal matter, I hope you will forgive me for not notifying you of my arrival."

"Of course," the Marquis answered. "Do sit down. I see my servants have brought you some refreshment."

The Earl had a glass of champagne in his hand. Now he put it on a side-table and did not sit, as the Marquis had suggested, but stood in front of the mantelpiece, as if he found what he had to say easier if he was on his feet.

The Marquis poured himself a small glass of champagne and waited, knowing that the Earl was finding it somewhat embarrassing to know how to start.

"I have been aware for some time, Alchester," he began at last, "that I should get married. As you will know, it is the wish of Their Majesties that those in constant attendance on them, like myself, should have a wife."

He paused. Then as the Marquis did not speak, he went on:

"My wife would of course be singularly fortunate in that she, as hereditary 'Lady of the Bedchamber,' would be not only a companion for Her Majesty but also a friend."

As the Earl continued standing, the Marquis seated himself in one of the armchairs and, crossing his legs, leant back.

He thought he was enjoying more than he had enjoyed anything for a long time seeing the Earl in the unaccustomed position of being, in effect, a sup-plicant.

"As the Queen is so young," the Earl continued, "twenty-six next birthday, it would therefore be pleas-ant for Her Majesty to have a younger person round her than she has at the moment. I am sure you will agree with me."

"Of course," the Marquis murmured.

"That is one reason why I have decided, after a great deal of thought and consideration, that I need a wife who is young in years, but naturally one who by birth and breeding qualified for the position she will hold not only at Court but as my wife."

Again he waited for the Marquis to speak, but he merely nodded his agreement and took another sip of champagne.

"It is not always easy to find exactly what one wants in life," the Earl said, "but I think that there is one young woman who I could say in all sincerity fulfils my requirements in almost every particular, and that, Alchester, is your Ward—Mirabelle Chester."

The Marquis gave a well-simulated start.

"Mirabelle!" he exclaimed. "But she has not yet made her debut."

"However, she is, I believe, eighteen," the Earl remarked.

"That is true, but I had not thought of her being married so quickly after her arrival in England."

"I cannot see any point in waiting."

The Marquis put down his glass.

"You have certainly taken me by surprise, Branscombe. Of course, as Mirabelle's Guardian I can see the advantages she would gain by marrying you, just as I can also see the advantages to you."

There was no need to say more, and he saw the flicker of greed in the Earl's eyes as he asked almost too casually for it to be natural:

"I believe she has a large fortune?"

"Very large!" the Marquis agreed. "In fact, an astronomical one, and it is likely to increase."

"Then I presume I have your permission," the Earl said with an undoubted note of triumph in his voice, "to pay my addresses to your Ward and ask for her hand in marriage?"

"Of course I cannot refuse such a request," the Marquis replied formally, "but there is one condition."

"Condition?"

"It is that since whoever Mirabelle marries will have the handling of her entire fortune when he marries her, I want my Ward to receive a certain sum of money from her bridegroom which will be hers unconditionally, and for life."

As he spoke, the Marquis thought he had phrased what he had said so cleverly that he had not in fact lied but had manipulated the words "Mirabelle" and "Ward" so that he spoke the truth.

He was aware that the Earl was looking at him in astonishment.

"What would be the point of that?" he enquired.

"I wish my Ward to feel independent of her husband."

"I assure you I will always be extremely generous."

"At the same time," the Marquis continued, "we all know of cases where a rich woman has been unable to obtain a penny of her own fortune once it became by marriage legally her husband's property."

"As I have said, I am known to be generous," the Earl boasted.

"I still have to safe-guard my Ward's interests," the Marquis persisted.

There was a little pause, then the Earl asked:

"How much are you proposing I should settle on her?"

"I was thinking, considering that Mirabelle's fortune is so colossal," the Marquis said, "that my Ward should receive on her wedding-day a capital sum which would bring her in a thousand pounds a year!"

"That is impossible!" the Earl snapped.

"Impossible?" the Marquis queried.

"I did not expect you to make such a strange request," the Earl said aggressively, "but as you have done so, I have to admit to you, of course in confidence, that it would be very difficult if not impossible for me to do what you ask."

"I find that incredible," the Marquis replied.

The Earl walked to the table where there was a bottle of champagne in a silver ice-bucket, and without asking permission he helped himself to another glass.

"I will be frank with you, Alchester," he said after he had drunk some of the champagne, "and explain something which few people know about, but which has left me in a somewhat embarrassing position."

The Marquis waited, thinking this was something he had not expected.

"My grandfather was a rich man," the Earl began, "but a very extravagant one. He also had a large family, all of whom he provided for in what my father, as the eldest son, thought was an over-generous manner."

The Marquis smiled slightly, knowing that it was traditional in aristocratic families that while the eldest son had everything, the younger members were usually kept on very short commons.

"My grandfather," the Earl continued, "was also, as I am, extremely proud of our ancestry. You will therefore understand that when Prince Frederick of Melderstein suggested that he should marry his youngest daughter, my grandfather was delighted."

The Marquis raised his eye-brows.

"I know Prince Frederick, but I had no idea that his wife was your aunt."

"She is not," the Earl said, "and that is the whole point of what I am telling you."

The way he spoke told the Marquis he did not like being interrupted, and he went on:

"The marriage was arranged, and because it was made quite obvious to my grandfather that the Prince expected a very large dowry with his bride, he behaved in what I consider a very reprehensible manner."

"What did he do?" the Marquis asked, already knowing the answer.

"He settled a considerable sum of money on my aunt, and, for some reason I have never been able to ascertain, made it over to her on the day before the wedding actually took place."

The Marquis was listening intently but he did not interrupt, and the Earl said dramatically:

"Then she disappeared!"

"Disappeared?"

"On the night before the wedding! As she took no possessions with her, it was thought at the time, and I still think so, that it was a case of foul play. She was obviously murdered!"

"But you have never been able to prove it?"

"How could we when there was no sign of her body?" the Earl asked sharply.

"And what this means," the Marquis said slowly, "is that you cannot touch the money that was settled on her by your grandfather."

"That is so," the Earl agreed. "At least the Courts informed me I cannot do so until after a lapse of twenty-five years. Then, I believe, she will be assumed dead and the money will revert to me."

"How much longer have you to wait?"

"Another five years or so."

The Marquis's lips twisted in what Peregrine would have thought was his cruel smile.

"I understand your predicament, Branscombe," he said, "but you will understand that in the light of

these unfortunate circumstances I could not give my
permission for you to marry my Ward."

"You would *refuse* me?"

The Earl's voice shook with astonishment.

"I am afraid so," the Marquis replied, "unless of
course you could scrape together enough money to
make my Ward independent."

He gave a little laugh.

"It should not be difficult to borrow any sum you
fancy on such expectations."

The Earl walked restlessly across the hearth-rug,
and, having drunk the champagne he had in his glass,
once again he helped himself.

The Marquis waited and finally the Earl said:

"If I settle enough to bring in your Ward five
hundred pounds a year, would you be satisfied?"

"Supposing we make it seven hundred fifty
pounds?" the Marquis suggested. "After all, with our
horses winning the Derby side by side, we should be
able to come to an amicable agreement on slightly
lower stakes."

The Earl thought for a moment. Then he said:

"Very well, but I consider you have driven a hard
bargain which I had not expected, Alchester."

"I am not thinking of you but of my Ward," the
Marquis replied. "I presume now you would like to
see her?"

"Of course," the Earl agreed. "And I would like
to suggest that the marriage take place without much
delay. I know that would please the Queen, and I
have my own reasons for not wishing to wait unnecessarily long before my marriage."

The Marquis had the idea that his reasons were
wholly financial, but he merely rang the bell and
when a footman appeared he said:

"Ask my Ward to join me."

"Very good, M'Lord."

As the door was shut again, the Earl said:

"I was thinking that I would like to introduce
Mirabelle to London as my wife, rather than have you
taking her there first as a débutante and then an-
nouncing our engagement."

The Marquis thought that the Earl must be in more urgent need of funds than he had intimated.

That he was in such a hurry certainly coincided with his own plans. But he had no intention of appearing too eager.

"Do you think that would be a good idea?" he asked. "Surely your relatives will think it very strange if they do not meet your future wife before you are married? And I suppose my own family would wish to meet you."

"I see no reason for those extremely boring family gatherings," the Earl said sharply. "What I think would be far easier for both of us would be for the marriage to take place here in your private Chapel, and then we can astound the Social World when it is a *fait accompli*."

"That is certainly something that commends itself to me," the Marquis said, "because if there is one thing I really dislike, it is a wedding. At the same time, it is something I would first wish to discuss with my Ward—and alone."

He thought as he spoke that if the Earl suggested a hasty marriage to Kistna without his preparing her for it, she might easily refuse to entertain such an idea. Worse still, she might give the whole game away.

The Earl had no time to acquiesce when the door opened and Kistna came in.

She was looking lovely, the Marquis decided at first glance. He also knew she was very frightened.

Her green gown was an elaborate and fashionable creation that was obviously extremely costly. Her hair was equally elaborate and she wore a tiny cluster of real snowdrops at her neck which made her look the embodiment of Spring.

She advanced towards them, the Marquis noted, at exactly the correct pace, stopping at the right place to curtsey. Then, with her eyes very wide, she looked only at him.

Because he knew how nervous she was, the Marquis took her hand in his and felt her fingers trembling like the wings of a captured bird.

He gave it a gentle pressure to give her confidence and said:

"I want to present, my dear, the Earl of Branscombe, who has asked if he may pay his addresses to you, and I can only commend him as a most suitable husband."

With difficulty the Marquis kept the sarcasm out of his voice.

The Earl bowed and there was no doubt that with his skilfully tied cravat, his close-fitting whipcord riding-coat, and his highly polished Hessian boots, he was a very handsome and fashionable man.

"Your Guardian, Miss Chester," he said to Kistna, "has given his permission to our union and I therefore have the honour to ask you to be my wife."

He put out his hand as he spoke, and the Marquis, feeling that Kistna was incapable of speech or movement, gave the hand he had been holding to the Earl.

He raised it to his lips.

"I feel sure," he said, "that we will deal extremely well together."

Still Kistna did not speak, and the Marquis said hastily:

"I think this calls for a glass of champagne, and I must of course drink your health."

He moved towards the table and poured champagne into two glasses, one for himself and one for Kistna.

He carried them back to where she was still standing, while the Earl had begun a monologue which made him sound more conceited with every word he spoke.

"As your Guardian will doubtless tell you," he said, "His Majesty relies on me greatly for advice and support, and the Queen asks my opinion on everything she does. It is a great responsibility and one which I hope my wife will share with me, just as I hope she will share the many demands made on me in Hampshire where the Branscombes have for many centuries played the leading part in County affairs."

The Marquis put a glass of champagne into Kistna's hand, then he raised his own to say:

"Let me drink to both of you! May you have many years of happiness!"

"Thank you," the Earl said.

He drained all the champagne that was left in his glass, while Kistna took only a tiny sip.

She was so pale that the Marquis thought suddenly that she was as white as the snowdrops at her neck, and he was afraid she might faint.

"Why do you not fetch Mr. Wallingham?" he suggested. "I am sure he would wish to hear the happy news."

"I ... I will ... do that," Kistna said in what seemed to be a strangled voice.

She put down her glass on the nearest table and hurried towards the door.

"She is young and shy," the Marquis explained, as if he felt he must make some excuse for her silence.

The Earl smiled.

"That is an attribute I find desirable in my future wife."

There was something in the way he spoke that made the Marquis want to hit him.

Then as he moved towards the bell to ask for more champagne, he was sure that Kistna would not return and he hoped that the Earl would not find such shyness suspicious.

As the Marquis had suspected, there was no sign of Kistna when Peregrine arrived to drink to the Earl's health and complimented him in such an insincere manner that he was forced to frown at him.

The Earl, however, was so supremely confident of his own importance that when he had finally driven away, the Marquis was quite sure he had never for one moment thought either that his suit would be rejected or that his future bride and her Guardian were not delighted at the idea of such an advantageous marriage.

"Blast him!" the Marquis said to Peregrine as they turned away from the front door. "I dislike him more every time I see him! All I can say is that if the

King can put up with Branscombe, he certainly should not jibe at the Reform Bill."

This was a point of bitter controversy in the Houses of Parliament and over the whole country, with the King making every possible excuse not to approve any of the reforms which were long over-due.

Peregrine, however, was not listening.

"What did Kistna think of him?" he asked.

"I have no idea, as she did not speak."

The Marquis had thought that in fact it was rather a good thing that she appeared so shy. At the same time, he thought it was unlike her, as she had too much character to behave in such a hesitant fashion.

"Where is she now?" Peregrine asked.

"Upstairs, I suppose," the Marquis replied. "I will send a servant to find her."

"If she is upset, perhaps it would be best for me to go and look for her," Peregrine suggested.

Then he hesitated and added:

"No—I think you should go. It will be you she wants to see."

The Marquis did not argue. He merely said:

"She will be in her Sitting-Room, I suppose, but I need a drink first. I cannot tell you how intolerable the Earl was, harping continually on his position at Court and of course his own importance."

"What have you done about Kistna's future?" Peregrine asked. "When he knows the truth, I am quite certain he will treat her as he treated Dulcie and chuck her out without a penny."

"I have thought of that," the Marquis said, "and I have given my consent only on condition that he settles a capital sum on her to bring in seven hundred fifty pounds a year."

His lips twisted before he added:

"I tried for a thousand, but Branscombe informed me that he was extremely short of money, and I even had to suggest that he borrow the money to provide the seven hundred fifty pounds on which we finally agreed."

"Why should he be so hard up?" Peregrine asked. "I always thought he was warm in the pocket."

"So did I," the Marquis agreed, "but apparently his grandfather, who was as big a snob as he is, settled a large sum on his aunt because she was to marry Prince Frederick of Melderstein. But she disappeared before the wedding, and although Branscombe is convinced that she was murdered, they have never been able to find the body."

"Now that you mention it," Peregrine said, "I remember my father telling me about that scandal. Apparently there was a tremendous commotion at the time because as it was a Royal Wedding, Crowned Heads had arrived from all over Europe."

He laughed.

"So not only the bride was lost, but so was the money which was settled on her! Can you imagine how much it must irk Branscombe not to be able to get his hands on it?"

"Now I know why he was so mad-keen to win the Derby," the Marquis said. "Apart from the honour and glory, two thousand eight hundred pounds is not to be sneezed at!"

"No, of course not," Peregrine agreed, "and he will try even harder for the Gold Cup. You will have to watch him, especially if he employs Jake Smith again."

"He had better not try any tricks at Ascot," the Marquis said. "If he does, I swear I will have both his horse and his jockey disqualified. I only wish I could disqualify him as well!"

"You will have punished him quite enough when he realises that Kistna has not a penny to her name."

"That, as I have now found out, will hurt even more than I thought it would," the Marquis said with satisfaction.

Then, as if speaking of Kistna brought her to mind, he said angrily:

"What the hell is she waiting for? Branscombe has gone, and I want to talk to her!"

Chapter Seven

"Dinner is served, M'Lord!"

The Marquis looked round at the Butler from the hearth-rug where he was standing talking to Peregrine.

"Miss Kistna is not down yet," he said sharply.

"Mrs. Dawes asked me to tell Your Lordship that Miss Kistna will not be coming down for dinner."

The Marquis did not reply, but there was a definite scowl between his eyes as he put down his glass and walked with Peregrine towards the Dining-Room.

When he had gone upstairs to speak to Kistna after the Earl had left, he had knocked on her door and it had been opened by Mrs. Dawes.

To the Marquis's surprise, she had stepped out into the passage, closing the door of the *Boudoir* behind her.

"I want to see Miss Kistna," the Marquis said sharply.

"I think, M'Lord, it'd be wise, if Your Lordship'll excuse me saying so, to leave her be," Mrs. Dawes answered. "She's upset at the moment and I'm trying to persuade her to lie down."

The Marquis's lips tightened.

There were several things he wanted to say, but not to Mrs. Dawes.

"Then tell Miss Kistna I shall be looking forward to seeing her at dinner," he replied.

Now when she refused to appear, he found himself feeling annoyed, although there was another emotion involved to which he did not wish to put a name.

Dinner as usual was excellent, but the Marquis helped himself absent-mindedly to the dishes he was offered, and his conversation with Peregrine was spasmodic, there being moments when they both sat in silence.

Finally when both gentlemen refused port and the servants left the room, the Marquis said:

"I have been thinking that my revenge on Branscombe will be even more effective than I expected. If he has to borrow the money I require for Kistna, he will doubtless have to pay a high rate of interest."

Peregrine did not reply and after a moment the Marquis said:

"You do not seem very elated. I thought you disliked Branscombe."

"I do," Peregrine replied, "but I do not like what your hatred of him is doing to you."

"Doing to me?" the Marquis asked in surprise.

Peregrine felt for words.

"My mother used to say that hatred is a boomerang that will come back to hurt the person who hates more than it hurts their victim."

"I understand what you are trying to tell me in a somewhah garbled manner," the Marquis said in a lofty tone. "At the same time, you can hardly expect me to let Branscombe get off scot-free, considering the way he behaved at the Derby."

Peregrine did not answer and the Marquis went on:

"I consider my plan to avenge myself very subtle, and, what is more, it will not only humiliate him but hurt him where he will mind it most—in his pocket!"

"I am sick of talking about him," Peregrine exclaimed irritably. "The whole thing is turning you into a monster, and I would rather Branscombe cheated his way to victory in a dozen Derbies rather than watch you plotting and intriguing in what I consider an extremely undignified manner."

The Marquis was astounded.

In all the years he had known Peregrine, when he had often thought they were as close in their friendship as if they were brothers, he had never been spoken to in such a manner.

He was just about to reply aggressively when he realised that the servants would be waiting for them to leave the Dining-Room and might conceivably overhear what they were saying.

Instead he rose to his feet, and as he did so he rang the gold hand-bell which stood on the table in front of him.

The door to the Pantry opened immediately.

"You rang, M'Lord?" the Butler enquired.

"Bring the decanter of brandy into the Library."

The Marquis walked from the Dining-Room, considering, as he went, how he could refute Peregrine's accusations and show him that he was being exceedingly unfair and was, to all intents and purposes, championing the Earl.

They reached the Library, where the Marquis preferred to sit if he was alone or had only masculine company.

Although it was not yet dusk, the candles were lit and the colourful leather-bound volumes decorating the walls up to the exquisitely painted ceiling showed to their best advantage in the soft light.

The Marquis, however, was intent on his own thoughts, and as the Butler set down the cut-glass decanter on the table beside the armchair, having first proferred a glass to Peregrine, the Marquis asked:

"I presume you have sent Miss Kistna her dinner upstairs?"

"I sent up the first course, M'Lord," the Butler replied, "but it was returned untouched with a message that the young lady did not require any dinner."

He left the Library as he finished speaking and the Marquis said angrily:

"I have never heard such nonsense! Of course she wants dinner when she is still weak from years of starvation!"

"She is obviously upset."

"Upset?" the Marquis questioned. "What has she to be upset about? I thought when I looked at Branscombe, obnoxious though we know him to be, he is quite a fine figure of a man from a woman's point of view."

"Presumably Kistna does not think so."

"Why should you say that?" the Marquis asked.

"I should have thought the answer to that question was obvious."

"Because she is sulking upstairs? What is the matter with the girl? God in Heaven, she has the chance of making the most brilliant marriage any woman could desire! She certainly has a better future than the one she had in mind of earning her own living."

"Is that what she suggested she should do?"

"She said something about it," the Marquis said vaguely. "Of course I told her the only qualifications she had were for working in an Orphanage, and I should have thought she had had enough of that."

"Really, Linden, such a remark was needlessly brutal!" Peregrine said scathingly.

Once again the Marquis looked at him in astonishment.

"I was attempting to make Kistna understand how fortunate she is. After all, she knows nothing about Branscombe. Why should she not want to marry him?"

There was silence. Then as the Marquis was obviously waiting for an answer, Peregrine, as if he was goaded into a reply, said:

"Why should she want to, when she loves—someone else?"

The Marquis's lips parted as if to question such a statement. Then the expression on his face changed and for a moment he just stood staring at Peregrine as if he had never seen him before.

Then abruptly without another word he went from the Library, slamming the door behind him.

He walked along the corridor, through the Hall, and up the Grand Staircase.

He moved forcefully and determinedly until he reached Kistna's *Boudoir,* where he stood still, as if he was considering what he should say, or perhaps questioning his own feelings.

Then he knocked.

There was no answer and he thought she must have gone to bed as Mrs. Dawes had wished her to do.

He went to the next door and knocked again. He heard a movement, then the door was opened and it was Mrs. Dawes who stood there.

When she saw the Marquis there was an expression of surprise on her face.

"I came to enquire how Miss Kistna is," he said. "I was worried when I heard she had refused to have any dinner."

"I thought Miss Kistna was with you, M'Lord."

The Marquis shook his head.

"I cannot understand it!" Mrs. Dawes exclaimed. "I was told downstairs that she had refused her dinner, and I thought she must be poorly, so I came up as soon as I'd finished my own meal, only to find the room empty."

As if he would see with his own eyes, the Marquis moved past the Housekeeper into the bedroom.

One glance told him that although the bed had been used, it was empty.

"When I came in a few minutes ago," Mrs. Dawes was saying, "I felt certain Miss Kistna had changed her mind and gone downstairs to Your Lordship. The wardrobe door was open, as Your Lordship can see, and I thought she must have put on one of her pretty gowns and done it up herself."

"She is not in the Library," the Marquis said, "and I can hardly imagine she would be sitting alone in the Salon."

"No, of course not, M'Lord," Mrs. Dawes replied. "But now I thinks of it—that could have been Miss Kistna!"

"What could?"

"I never thought it at the time," Mrs. Dawes said, "but when I came into the bedroom a short time ago I realised the curtains had not been pulled, so I went to the window. As I did so, I thinks I sees someone in white crossing the lawn towards the lake."

"I cannot believe Miss Kistna would want to go there at this time of the night," the Marquis said.

"She might have thought she needed a little fresh air," Mrs. Dawes answered. "She was upset, very upset, M'Lord, and it's not good for her to be in such a state when she's still so weak from what she went through in that terrible place."

"No, of course not," the Marquis agreed.

"I've never known her so unhappy, M'Lord. It broke my heart to see her. It was almost as if she'd had bad news."

The Marquis was aware that Mrs. Dawes was consumed with curiosity. Then as he did not reply, she said:

"If I was you, M'Lord, I'd see if I could find her. It's not right for her to be walking about in the dark, and in the state she's in. Accidents can happen at night."

The Marquis looked sharply at the Housekeeper. Then without saying a word he went from the bedroom.

He did not return by the way he had come down the Grand Staircase, where footmen were on duty in the Hall, but instead went very quickly down the corridor to where there was a secondary staircase.

This led to the East Wing of the great house, where there was a door which opened directly onto the garden.

It was locked, but it took the Marquis only a few moments to turn the key and pull back the two bolts. Then he was out on the lawn which stretched from the house down to the lake.

He realised, from what Mrs. Dawes had said, that the person she thought might be Kistna had been moving towards the end of the lake which was obscured from the house by trees and shrubs.

It was strange, he thought, that she should be going in that particular direction. Then a sudden idea came to him which made him quicken his pace.

It came back to his mind how as they were crossing the bridge which spanned the lake, Kistna had looked down at the sunshine playing on the water and asked:

"Do you ever swim here? I am sure you must have done so when you were a boy."

"Very often," the Marquis had replied with a smile, "but only in this part. The other end is dangerous."

"Why?" Kistna had enquired.

"It has what the gardeners call 'shifting sands,'" the Marquis had replied. "There are certain undercurrents as well, and a man was drowned there many years ago. My father put it out-of-bounds to me and to everybody else."

"I am sure you obeyed him," Kistna had said laughingly.

"Of course," the Marquis had replied. "I was a model child!"

Now the light-hearted conversation came back to him in a sinister way, but he told himself that even to entertain such an idea was quite ridiculous.

At the same time, he began to move faster, and now as he reached first the banks of shrubs, then the almond and cherry trees which, covered in blossom, were very beautiful, he began to move even quicker.

He tried to tell himself that the white figure Mrs. Dawes thought she had seen was undoubtedly the white lilac, or perhaps, as it was growing dusk, it was merely the petals lying on the ground which had given the illusion of there being a figure.

Yet, because he was afraid, he began to run.

He had forgotten what a long way it was to the end of the lake and how thick the lilac and syringa had grown in the past years.

Then when he was feeling breathless and, despite being extremely fit, his heart seemed to be pounding in his breast, he emerged through a thick belt of trees to see the end of the lake—and Kistna.

He was relieved that she was there and at the same time was almost embarrassed by his own fears, and he came to a standstill in the shelter of the trees and stood looking at her.

He saw that she was standing where the bank was high above a pool at the spot which was considered dangerous and where the man had been drowned.

Kistna appeared to be bending over. The Marquis was unable to see what she was doing and thought she must be picking flowers, which seemed odd at this time of the evening.

Then he saw that on the bank beside her was something large and bulky.

He stared, wondering what it could be, and in the faint light coming from the last of the sunset he realised that it was a brown linen bag.

He recognised it as being one of the laundry bags in which the housemaids collected the sheets and towels which were to be taken downstairs to be washed.

The Marquis wondered why Kistna had brought the bag with her.

Then he saw that now she was bending down to tie something round her ankles.

He stared as she knotted it several times before he saw that there was a cord attached to the bag.

Kistna straightened herself and turned to look at the water beneath her. With a shock of sheer horror the Marquis realised what she intended to do.

He reached her in a few strides, and when he was beside her and his hands went out to take hold of her, she gave a little cry.

"No...no! Go...away! Leave me alone...you are not to...stop me!"

She tried to struggle with him as she spoke, and he knew that she was standing on the very edge of the pool and that with one unwary movement she would topple over and into the water.

He held her close against him and tried to lift her to safety but found that the heavy bag to which her ankles were attached made her immobile. He guessed then that it contained stones.

"How could you think of doing anything so wrong—so wicked?" he asked.

"I cannot ... help it," she answered.

"Of course you can," he scolded.

His voice was raw because he had been so afraid.

"If you had only come a ... few seconds later ..." she whispered, "it would have been too ... late ... I would not be here ... and no-one would ever have ... found me."

The Marquis's arms tightened about her. Then he said:

"Why should you want to do anything so crazy and so utterly and completely mad?"

He was still holding her close against him and she made an impulsive little movement as if, despite his being there, she would still do as she had intended and drown herself.

The Marquis's arms held her still, and as if she knew that any further struggle would be futile, she suddenly went limp and her head rested against his shoulder.

"I do not understand," he said. "How could you even think of anything so terrible?"

"Papa would have ... thought it ... wicked of me," Kistna said in a voice he could barely hear, "but ... Mama ... would have ... understood."

"What would she have understood?" the Marquis asked, as if he were speaking to a child.

"That I ... I cannot ... marry that man! He is ... bad ... I knew it when he ... touched my ... h-hand."

"Bad?" the Marquis questioned. "Why should you say that?"

"I am ... sure of it. There is ... something about ... him ... something that made me ... afraid ... and besides ... I cannot ... m-marry anyone!"

"Why not?"

He saw that she was about to reply. Then, as if she realised to whom she was speaking, she turned her face and hid it against him.

"I want you to answer that question," the Marquis said, and his voice was gentle.

"N-no . . . I . . . cannot . . . tell . . . you."

The Marquis put his fingers under her chin and turned her face up to his.

"Look at me, Kistna!" he said. "Look at me and tell me why you cannot marry anyone!"

As he looked down at her, he could see the unhappiness in her eyes and the tear-stains on her cheeks.

It seemed to him for a moment as if she looked as pathetic and miserable as she had when he had first seen her.

Yet, with her body close against his, he knew that during the time she had been at the Abbey she had changed and become very different from the miserable, starving creature who he had thought at first was so ugly.

Now she had a beauty that was different from anything he had seen in any other woman, and as he felt her trembling because of his questions, he knew that never before in his whole life had he felt as he was feeling now.

Because she was so young and because she had come to him from the Orphanage, it had never struck the Marquis that Kistna was a desirable woman, like Isobel or any of the other women with whom he had amused himself.

He had been so intent on educating her and preparing her to be the Earl's wife that he had not thought of her as a human being but merely as an instrument he could use to injure the man he hated.

Now as she looked up at him and he saw her answer in the depths of her expressive eyes, and as he was aware that she was quivering against him, not from fear but because he was touching her, he felt a strange rapture sweep over him.

"Tell me," he said, and now his voice was very soft and beguiling, "tell me why you say you will never be married and why you cannot marry the Earl."

He knew that the deep note in his voice and the nearness of him affected her. Then, as if he took her will away from her and it was impossible for her to withstand him, her eyes looked into his, and in a broken little voice that was very near to tears she whispered:

"I . . . I . . . love you . . . I . . . c-cannot . . . help it . . . I love . . . you . . . how could I . . . let . . . another . . . man . . . t-touch me?"

"No other man shall!"

His lips were on hers.

He felt her stiffen as if from sheer shock, then she surrendered herself to the insistence of his kiss.

He did not know a woman's mouth could be so soft, sweet, innocent, and yet at the same time so exciting in a way he had never known before.

As his arms tightened round her, the Marquis knew that he had found something he had always been seeking. While it had eluded him and he was not quite certain what it was, he had known that it was there, only out of reach.

Now it was his and he recognised it as love, the real love that had nothing in common with the fiery but easily quenched passion he had known with so many other women.

To Kistna it was as if the Heavens had opened, and the Marquis, who she had identified long ago as St. Michael, carried her up into the divine light which she had always been aware was part of love.

She heard music and there were the songs of angels combined with the scent of flowers.

This was the ultimate wonder, the beauty she had always looked for but which in all its perfection could only come to her through somebody she loved.

She knew that she loved the Marquis as her mother had loved her father, and his lips holding her captive gave her a beauty which was a part of God.

When the Marquis raised his head, she said in a voice that vibrated with the rapture he had aroused in her:

"I . . . I love you . . . and what I . . . wanted before I . . . died was for you to . . . kiss me. . . ."

"How can you wish to die when you belong to me?" he asked. "And I know now that I can never lose you—never let you go!"

It seemed for a moment as if the last rays of the sun lit her face, and she stammered:

"D-do you . . . mean I can . . . stay with you . . . and not have to . . . m-marry. . . ?"

"You will marry me!" the Marquis said firmly.

The start she gave told him that the idea had never crossed her mind, and he said:

"You must try to forgive me, my darling, for having been so absurdly blind, so stupid as not to realise until now that I love you and you are everything I want my wife to be."

"Do you . . . mean that . . . do you really mean it?"

"I love you!" the Marquis said simply.

He was kissing her again, kissing her with long, slow, demanding kisses which seemed to Kistna to draw her soul from between her lips so that she became his and she was no longer herself but part of him. . . .

* * *

A long time later, when the first stars were coming out overhead, the Marquis said in a voice which sounded strange and very unlike his own:

"I think, my precious one, we should move from this very precarious position. If you fell into the lake now, we might both be drowned!"

Kistna gave a little cry of horror.

"You must be careful . . . very careful."

The Marquis smiled.

"That is what I should be saying to you, to stand very still and hold on to me while I untie that rope from round your ankles."

As he spoke he bent down and released her, then he picked up the linen sack, which was in fact very heavy, and threw it into the water.

As it splashed and sank out of sight, the Marquis knew with a shudder that if he had been just a few seconds later it would have been impossible to save Kistna and she would have drowned as she had intended.

Nobody would ever have known what had happened to her, and it was doubtful if her body would ever have been recovered.

As if he was afraid even to think of anything so horrifying, he lifted her in his arms and carried her away from the water's edge towards the trees.

"I ought to be very, very angry with you!" he said.

"P-please forgive me," Kistna pleaded. "It was ... only because I ... loved you so ... desperately ... that I would rather ... die than leave you."

"You will never leave me!" the Marquis said. "I know now, as I should have known long ago, that I cannot contemplate life without you."

"I thought," she said in a low voice, "that if you ... would love me ... for a month ... a week ... even a d-day ... I would be ... grateful and try to ask for ... nothing more."

"I intend that you shall have a great deal more," the Marquis replied. "Me, for instance, as long as we both shall live!"

Kistna gave a little cry.

"That is what I want, to be with you ... to love you and be in ... Heaven."

The Marquis set her down on the ground in the shade of an almond tree.

"If Heaven is here on earth," he said, "that is what I shall give you, but you will have to make it a Heaven for me too."

"That is what it will be ... if you are ... there," Kistna answered, and lifted her lips to his. ...

Later they walked slowly back to the house, taking a long time over it.

Everything Kistna said seemed to the Marquis to invite her kisses, and when they stepped out of the darkness into the light, he thought that love had given her a beauty that was like the sun. She radiated a happiness which was linked with the vibrations coming from himself.

Holding hands, they walked into the Library to find Peregrine asleep in an armchair with the *Times* on his knees.

But before they could speak his name, as if in his dreams he sensed their presence, his eyes opened and he jerked himself into wakefulness.

"Where have you been. . . . ?" he began.

Then as he saw the expressions on their faces, he gave a cry and rose to his feet.

"What has happened?" he asked, knowing it was an unnecessary question.

It was Kistna who answered him—Kistna who looked so different from the way she had ever looked before that it was hard to recognise her.

"We are . . . to be . . . married!" she said, and it was a paean of happiness.

Peregrine gave a cry of delight and flung the *Times* high in the air.

"Hoorah!" he cried. "That is what I hoped! Congratulations, Linden! I thought sooner or later you would see sense!"

"Sense?" the Marquis questioned. "Is that what you call it?"

He spoke lightly, then turned to smile at Kistna, and as Peregrine saw the expression in his eyes, he knew that all he wanted for his friend had come true.

After a great many false starts and a number of disappointments, the Marquis had won the race for love which had always eluded him.

Peregrine knew as they looked at each other that he was for the moment forgotten and that he intruded on something so beautiful that it was almost a shock when he said:

"We must drink to this! May I order a bottle of champagne?"

"I think it is more important that Kistna has something to eat," the Marquis said.

"I am too happy to be hungry," she replied.

"Nevertheless, because it is good for you I want you to eat something to please me."

"You know I would do . . . anything that . . . pleases you," she said in a low voice.

They were standing close to each other and once again they were looking into each other's eyes as if they spoke without words and could hardly believe the glory they found there.

"You rang, M'Lord?" the Butler asked from the door.

With an effort the Marquis came back to reality.

"Ask the Chef to prepare a light supper for Miss Kistna, and bring a bottle of champagne."

"Very good, M'Lord."

The Butler was just about to shut the door when there was a footman at his side and he took from the man a silver salver on which there reposed a letter and brought it to the Marquis.

"This arrived, M'Lord, a few minutes ago. It reached the Post Office, I understand, too late to be delivered at the usual time, but as it is marked 'Urgent' and comes from abroad, the Post Master sent his son up to the house with it."

The Marquis took the letter from the salver.

"Thank him," he said to the Butler, "and reward the boy."

"I'll see to it, M'Lord."

The Marquis, looking down at the letter, said with a smile:

"It is from Rome and it must therefore concern my Ward, Mirabelle."

He smiled at Kistna and added:

"There is no need now, my darling, for you to have to impersonate her or anybody else. All I want is that you should be you, and my wife!"

"H-how soon can we be . . . m-married?"

"I have no intention of waiting for one moment longer than is necessary," the Marquis replied. "Nor do I intend to have a large and fashionable wedding."

Kistna gave a little cry.

"Oh, no, please . . . we want nobody there but . . . ourselves."

"And Peregrine," the Marquis added. "He will have to give you away, and be Best Man and our witness!"

"Thank you," Peregrine said wryly. "I am only

surprised you do not wish me to play the organ as well!"

"I would make you do that if I thought you were capable of it!" the Marquis teased.

"Of course we want him at our wedding," Kistna said.

Then she looked at the Marquis and said almost nervously:

"It is . . . true? It is really . . . true that you will . . . marry me?"

"Very true!" the Marquis said definitely.

Then as if he could not help himself he put his arm around her and drew her close to him.

She put her cheek in a caressing little gesture against his shoulder. Then as if she was embarrassed by her own emotions she said:

"Open the letter. After all, it is marked 'Urgent.'"

As she spoke she was afraid that it might contain something which would prevent the Marquis from being married as soon as he intended.

As if he too felt anxious, the Marquis walked to his desk and, picking up his gold and jewelled letter-opener, slit the envelope and drew out a thin sheet of paper.

He read it while Kistna watched him with eyes which Peregrine thought expressed her love very eloquently.

The Marquis finished the letter and looked up and smiled.

"They say that lightning never strikes twice," he said, "but obviously one marriage breeds another!"

"What has happened?" Peregrine enquired.

"Mirabelle's aunt writes to tell me that she has fallen in love with the young Prince di Borghese, and he with her. As he is an extremely rich young man, there is no question of his being interested only in her fortune, and she therefore hopes I will give my permission for them to become engaged and for the marriage to take place before the end of the summer."

The Marquis put out his hand towards Kistna.

"I think, my darling," he said, "you and I might include Rome in our honeymoon tour and attend my Ward's wedding, which will be very different in every way from ours."

"Our honeymoon!" Kistna murmured, feeling that word was more important to her than anything else the Marquis had said.

"Our honeymoon abroad," the Marquis said with a smile. "I want us to be alone, which would be difficult in England, where everybody will want to meet you."

Kistna gave a little cry.

"Then please . . . please . . . let us go abroad . . . I want to be . . . alone with you."

The way she spoke was very moving, and the Marquis threw the letter down on his desk and put his arms round her.

"We will be married the day after tomorrow," he said firmly. "I will send Anderson to London to get a Special Licence, and before anyone is aware of what has happened we will be on our way to Paris!"

"No, to . . . Heaven!" Kistna said softly. "Our Heaven . . . yours and mine."

* * *

The room in which they had dinner was small but very attractive. As Kistna had said when she first saw it, the small Manor the Marquis owned a little way off the Dover Road was just like a doll's house.

"What can you want with a house there, when you have the Abbey?" she had asked when the Marquis told her where they would spend the first night of their honeymoon.

"I keep a change of horses on the Dover Road, and I prefer them to be in my own stables rather than in those of a Posting Inn."

"You are very grand!" she teased.

"No—practical," he answered. "I must have known, through some inner sense, that one day the Manor would be a perfect place in which to start our honeymoon."

They had been married in the Chapel at the Abbey and it had seemed to Kistna redolent with the faith of ages.

She fancied that the monks who had first worshipped there were joining in the prayers said by the Marquis's Chaplain and that she could hear their deep voices behind the music of the organ.

It was on Peregrine's arm that she had walked into the Chapel to find the Marquis waiting for her.

"Mrs. Dawes says it is unlucky for a bridegroom to see his future wife on their wedding-day, before the service," Kistna had said, "and I want to be very, very lucky, so I will just stay in my room until I meet you in the Chapel."

"You have brought me luck already," the Marquis replied. "I have never felt so happy, so content, or so excited about the future."

"That is what I want you to feel. But supposing I . . . bore you, as I have been told you have been . . . bored by so many . . . beautiful women?"

"What I feel for you is very different," the Marquis said firmly, and knew that was the truth.

Now as he looked at Kistna across the small table which had been decorated with white flowers, he wondered, as he had a thousand times already, how he had not recognised her as his ideal from the moment they had first met.

In the candlelight, wearing a white gown with real orange-blossoms in her hair, she looked so lovely, and the very embodiment of youth, beauty, and happiness, that the Marquis thought only music could describe her adequately.

"I love you!" he said.

As if there were no other words that could express what they were both feeling, Kistna replied:

"I love . . . you . . . but I also . . . worship you because to me you have always seemed to be . . . St. Michael . . . who came to rescue me from the darkness of Hell and lift me into the light of Heaven."

"My precious!" the Marquis said in his deep voice.

Then as if he could not bear there to be a table between them, he stretched out his hands to draw her to her feet.

They walked from the Dining-Room, where they had sat for a long time, up the twisting oak staircase to the old-fashioned bedroom with its oak four-poster bed.

The room was lit by only three candles on a small table beside the blue-curtained bed, and Kistna was aware that neither her maid nor the Marquis's valet was waiting up for them.

As the Marquis shut the door behind him, she felt an excitement seep over her which he thought once again gave her a beauty that was so exquisite and so spiritual that it could only be part of the Divine.

Then as his arms went round her and his lips sought her, he knew that their love was very human.

He kissed her passionately, demandingly, before he said:

"I adore you! But I will try to remember how young you are and that I must not frighten you, my precious little love."

"I shall never be frightened by you except when you are ... angry with me," Kistna answered. "You love me and I know that everything you do is perfect and part of God."

"My darling, my wonderful little wife, I adore you."

Then the Marquis was kissing her until there was no need for words and the light of love enveloped them until they were dazzled by the glory of it.

* * *

A long time later, when the candles were guttering low, Kistna said:

"I have just remembered something!"

"What is it, my precious?" the Marquis answered.

Then as he looked at her lying against his shoulder he put out his hand to touch her hair.

"How can you be so beautiful?"

"You are . . . quite sure you still . . . think so?"

He smiled.

"Every moment I am with you, every time I touch you," he answered, "you seem more beautiful, more adorable, until I am afraid."

"Afraid?" she asked.

"That you might tire of me!"

She gave a little laugh of sheer happiness.

"That is the most marvellous compliment you could pay me, and when I think of how I looked when you rescued me, words like that are a present of the stars, the moon, and the sun, and no woman could ask for more."

"There are so many things I want to give you," the Marquis said, "but I agree that they could not compare with the stars, the moon, and the sun!"

He pulled her closer, and with his lips against the softness of her skin he said:

"I love you: the things you say, your quick little mind, your soft voice, and your eyes! And as Peregrine said once, you have the most adorable little nose."

"Peregrine said that?" Kistna enquired.

"He said a great many things about you," the Marquis replied, "but if you allow him to flirt with you or you become too fond of him, I shall be jealous."

"There is . . . no need for you to feel jealous of anyone," she said, and now there was a passionate note in her voice. "I love you . . . and now that you have taught me how perfect and beautiful love can be, you can understand there is . . . no other man in the whole world . . . but you."

The Marquis would have kissed her, but she said:

"I was telling you what I have remembered, and it is something I must do on my wedding-day."

"What is it?"

"I promised Mama that when I was married I would open a letter she gave me."

"A letter?" the Marquis questioned.

Kistna's voice was low as she said:

"I think Mama had a presentiment that she and Papa might die from the cholera."

The Marquis pulled her closer to him as she went on:

"There were only a few cases at first, but the authorities were worried, and of course Papa insisted on doing everything he could to help."

Kistna paused, as if she was looking back into the past.

"One day Mama sat for a long time writing at her desk. Then she said to me: 'Bring me your Bible, the one Papa gave you.'

"I fetched it from my bedroom and she very carefully opened the leather cover where it was attached inside."

"Why did she do that?" the Marquis asked.

"She slipped the letter she had written into it and sealed it," Kistna answered. "Then Mama said: 'I do not want you to read this or even think about it until you are married. Then, on your wedding-day, open it, unless I have told you in the meantime what the letter contains.'"

"You must have been curious," the Marquis remarked.

"I was, in a way," Kistna answered, "but it did not seem very important and Mama never spoke of it again."

"But the Bible has always been with you."

"I told you, it is the only possession I have."

"Very well," the Marquis said. "Open it now, before I prevent you from doing so."

He kissed her shoulder as he spoke, and she pushed the curtain aside and reached out to take her Bible, which was on the table beside the candles.

Then she sat up in bed and the Marquis lay back against the pillows, watching her.

He thought it would be impossible to find anyone so lovely and so attractive and at the same time so completely unselfconscious and so sensitive.

He knew it was not only her love but also an intuition which most young girls did not have which made her responsive to everything he asked of her.

He realised when he made love to her that he had found in one very young woman the completion of himself.

Because he loved her and was thinking more of her feelings than of his own, they had both been aroused spiritually as well as physically to an ecstasy which was to the Marquis an experience he had never known before and which seemed to him perfect in every way.

He knew now that his love for Kistna, which he had been so stupid not to recognise at first, had already deepened and developed until he was confident that he would make her as happy as she made him.

As he looked at her he thought that no other woman could arouse him as she did.

Nor had he ever known before a physical satisfaction combined with a spiritual rapture which ignited within him ideals and new ambitions which he was aware would, in the future, enrich his life.

Kistna had drawn the closely written sheets of paper from the cover of her Bible.

She opened the folded sheets and the Marquis knew there was an expression of sadness in her eyes as she thought of her mother.

He felt as if she moved away from him, and instinctively he put out his hand to touch her.

As if she understood, she turned her head and smiled at him.

"Shall I read you what Mama says?" she asked. "I want to share this with you as we share everything else."

"Of course, my precious."

Kistna held the letter so that the light from the candles shone on it, and in her soft, musical voice she read:

"*My dearest, most beloved daughter:*
Just in case anything should ever happen to me, I want to tell you a secret about which I have no wish to speak to you at the moment, and especially in front of Papa.

You know how happy we have been together, your father and I, and how I am the most fortunate woman in the world to love and be loved by a man who is so wonderful in every way that he could only have been sent to me by God. But, Kistna, to marry your father I had to do what most people would·have said was a very reprehensible act, although it was a courageous one.

I have never talked to you about my family because it was too dangerous for Papa's sake for me to do so.

Had my father been able to find him, I know, because he was a very powerful and in many ways a vindictive man, he would have made us both suffer, and perhaps he would even have destroyed Papa."

As if she was astonished by what she had just read, Kistna looked quickly at the Marquis as if the very sight of him gave her comfort and a feeling of security.

"Go on, my precious one," he said gently, and she continued:

"'My father was in fact the seventh Earl of Branscombe! I was his younger daughter, and I think without conceit he was fonder of me than of any of his other children. He was therefore very proud when Prince Frederick of Melderstein asked for my hand in marriage.

Needless· to say, I was not consulted as to whether or not I wished to marry him. I was just told how fortunate I was and that I should be overwhelmed with gratitude at the thought of wearing a Royal Crown. ·

I too might have thought it would be an advantageous position in life, had I not already fallen in love so overwhelmingly, so completely, that for me there was no other man in the whole world."

Kistna gave a little cry.

"That is what I feel for you," she said to the Marquis.

"I will tell you what I feel for you, my lovely one," he replied, "but finish the letter."

Kistna continued:

> "I had met your father when I was arranging the flowers in the Church. It was something I did every Saturday and it was one of the tasks that had been allotted to me for several years.
>
> He introduced himself as being the new Curate, and we talked, and after that we met every week, although of course my father and mother had no idea of it.
>
> And because, as you yourself see, he is so handsome and so very, very lovable, I fell wildly in love with him and I knew, although he said nothing, that he loved me too.
>
> When I was told that my father had agreed I should marry Prince Frederick, we both broke down and confessed what we felt for each other, but we knew it was hopeless.
>
> Your father said he could not bear to stay in Europe when I was married to the Prince, so he arranged through one of his relatives in the East India Company to go out to India as a Missionary.
>
> It was known that the ban on Missionary work in India was to be lifted, and because your Papa was so eager to get away, his relative agreed to help him with the fare so that he could go before the other Missionaries had their passages arranged for them.
>
> It was not of your father's choosing, but he learnt that the ship in which he was to sail would leave Tilbury the morning of my wedding-day.
>
> By the time I was beside myself at the thought of losing your father and being forced to marry the Prince, I found it impossible to take any interest in my trousseau, the presents, or the expensive preparations that were being made for my wedding.
>
> Then when the moment came to say good-bye, I knew it was impossible to live without your father, and if I could not be with him, I would rather die."

Kistna glanced at the Marquis and she knew what they were both thinking. Then she went on reading:

"We met in the Church, which was already decorated with the white flowers for my wedding-ceremony the next day. Your father was dressed in his travelling-clothes, and he was to catch the stage-coach which stopped at the cross-roads near the village, at five o'clock that evening.

When we met, I knew that I could not let him go. 'Take me with you!' I begged. 'Please take me with you! If you leave me behind, I will kill myself, because I cannot marry anyone but you!'

For a moment your father did not believe me. Then when he realised that I spoke the truth from the very depths of my heart, he put his arms round me and I knew that I need no longer be afraid and the future was ours!

I went with your father on the stage-coach just as I was. I did not go back to the house for anything in case they should stop me from leaving. We were married early in the morning by a very old Parson, who, fortunately, when I told him I was older than I was, was too blind to see clearly. We went aboard the ship together and nobody troubled about two unimportant missionaries.

We learnt a long time later that there had been a terrible commotion over my disappearance on the night before the wedding and that it was suspected that I had been murdered. I was only glad that everyone should think that and not search for me, for otherwise your father might have been accused of abducting a minor or, worst of all, my father might have tried to annul the marriage.

When you read this, dearest little Kistna, it will mean I am no longer with you. But remember that I have been the happiest woman in the world because I was married to the man I loved, who loved me and who gave me the crown of love which is more valuable than anything else.

Bless you, my darling, and I hope that as

*this is your marriage-night you will find the same
happiness that I have had, the same marvellous
love which will keep and protect you all through
your life.*"

Kistna's voice broke on the last words. Then she
put down the letter and the Marquis pulled her into
his arms.

"Your mother and father loved as we love," he
said, "and we will be as happy as they were."

Vaguely at the back of his mind he knew that the
revenge he had wanted on the Earl of Branscombe
was complete, and that because he could prove that
the money the seventh Earl had settled on his daughter was now Kistna's, he would remain financially
handicapped until he could find another heiress.

It was poetic justice, but it did not matter and the
Marquis knew that his revenge was quite unimportant.

What mattered was that he had found Kistna,
and love.

She had changed his life and he knew he was not
the same man, nor would he ever revert to being hard,
ruthless, and, as Peregrine had said, "a monster"
again.

He was wildly, deliriously happy and he wanted
other people to be happy too. Perhaps not the Earl—
that was too much to expect!

But at least he no longer felt vindictive towards
him, nor would he allow him to sour his feelings in
the future as he had in the past.

As far as he was concerned, the only thing that
mattered was Kistna's happiness, and he knew because she loved him it was in his power to give it to
her.

There were tears in her eyes now because she
was moved by what she had read, and the Marquis
kissed them away.

Then he kissed her little nose and her lips.

He kissed her until her sadness vanished and he
knew that the fire that was rising within himself had

ignited a flame within her that had flickered when he had made love to her before.

Now it was more intense, and as his lips moved over the softness of her neck and she quivered against him, he knew that he evoked in her new sensations she had not experienced before.

"I love ... you," she whispered breathlessly, "and you ... excite me."

"As you excite me," the Marquis replied. "I want you—God, how I want you!"

"I am ... yours ... oh, love me ... love me!"

Then as his hands touched her, and his lips held hers once again captive, and as his heart beat against hers, he knew she believed that he was St. Michael carrying her up towards the glory of Heaven.

He felt as if they touched the stars, the sun was burning within them, and a light enveloped them.

Then there was only love and they were one.

ABOUT THE AUTHOR

BARBARA CARTLAND, the world's most famous romantic novelist, who is also an historian, playwright, lecturer, political speaker and television personality, has now written over 200 books.

She has also had many historical works published and has written four autobiographies as well as the biographies of her mother and that of her brother Ronald Cartland, who was the first Member of Parliament to be killed in the last war. This book has a preface by Sir Winston Churchill.

Barbara Cartland has sold 100 million books over the world, more than half of these in the U.S.A. She broke the world record in 1975 by writing twenty books, and her own record in 1976 with twenty-one. In addition, her album of love songs has just been published, sung with the Royal Philharmonic Orchestra.

In private life, Barbara Cartland, who is a Dame of the Order of St. John of Jerusalem, has fought for better conditions and salaries for Midwives and Nurses. As President of the Royal College of Midwives (Hertfordshire Branch), she has been invested with the first Badge of Office ever given in Great Britain which was subscribed to by the Midwives themselves. She has also championed the cause for old people and founded the first Romany Gypsy Camp in the world.

Barbara Cartland is deeply interested in Vitamin Therapy and is President of the British National Association for Health.

Barbara Cartland

The world's bestselling author of romantic fiction. Her stories are always captivating tales of intrigue, adventure and love.

☐	13556	LOVE IN THE CLOUDS	$1.50
☐	13035	LOVE CLIMBS IN	$1.50
☐	13126	TERROR IN THE SUN	$1.50
☐	13579	FREE FROM FEAR	$1.75
☐	13832	LITTLE WHITE DOVES OF LOVE	$1.75
☐	13907	THE PERFECTION OF LOVE	$1.75
☐	13827	BRIDE TO THE KING	$1.75
☐	13910	PUNISHED WITH LOVE	$1.75
☐	13830	THE DAWN OF LOVE	$1.75
☐	13942	LUCIFER AND THE ANGEL	$1.75
☐	14084	OLA AND THE SEA WOLF	$1.75
☐	14133	THE PRUDE AND THE PRODIGAL	$1.75
☐	13984	LOVE FOR SALE	$1.75

Barbara Cartland's NEW Magazine

Barbara Cartland's
World of Romance

If you love Barbara Cartland books, you'll feel the same way about her new magazine. *Barbara Cartland's World of Romance* is the new monthly that contains an illustrated Cartland novel, the story behind the story, Barbara's personal message to readers, and many other fascinating and colorful features.

You can save $4.73 with an introductory 9-month subscription. Pay only $8.77 for 9 issues—a $13.50 value.

So take advantage of this special offer and subscribe today using the handy coupon below. <u>For less than 98¢ an issue, you can receive nine months of the best in romantic fiction.</u>

SUBSCRIPTION ORDER FORM

Yes, I want to subscribe to *Barbara Cartland's World of Romance*. I have enclosed $8.77 (check or money order), the special introductory price for nine issues of the best in romantic fiction. (Canadian subscribers add $1.00, $9.77 for nine issues.)

Name_____

Address_____

City_____State_____Zip_____

Send to: Barbara Cartland's World of Romance
      57 West 57th Street
      New York, N.Y. 10019

NO RISK: If you don't like your first copy for any reason, cancel your subscription and keep the first issue FREE. Your money will be refunded in full.
        This offer expires September 1981.

BG-4